The Girls

Also by Helen Yglesias

FICTION

How She Died
Family Feeling
Sweetsir
The Saviors

NONFICTION

Starting: Early, Anew, Over, and Late
Isabel Bishop
Semblant

The Girls

HELEN YGLESIAS

DELPHINIUM BOOKS

Harrison, New York   Encino, California

Library of Congress Cataloging-in-Publication Data
Yglesias, Helen.
The girls/Helen Yglesias. — 1st ed.
p.   cm
ISBN 1-883285-16-X (alk. paper)
I. Title.
PS3575.G48G57   1999
813'.54—dc21   99-24670
                                       CIP

First Edition
10 9 8 7 6 5 4 3 2 1

Distributed by HarperCollins*Publishers*
Printed in the United States of America on acid-free paper
Designed by Krystyna Skalski

This book is for my sisters.

The Girls

1

THEIRAMI

It had been the little kids in the family who heard Miami as Theirami—Grandma and Grandpa's Ami, Aunt Naomi's Ami, Aunt Eva's Ami, Uncle Max's Ami, all the way down the Witkovsky family line. That was fine with Jenny. Their Ami, not hers. Jenny had never wanted any part of Anybody's Ami. She was glad that her own children had never claimed the place.

They had been a large family, seven brothers and sisters plus Mama and Papa: four girls, as they were still called into their nineties, "the girls," and three boys, "the boys" into their eighties. The males died younger, died, in Miami, one after the other, though Mama went first; then Lionel, out of the family order, a middle brother; then Papa; then the eldest brother, Stanley; and recently powerful Max, dead of prostate cancer as if he were any old body and not the head of a huge moneymaking industry—clothing factories, retail stores, real estate, investment banking. Philanthropy, of course. Dead anyway, before his two older sisters and his two younger, leaving only Mama and Papa's four daughters still to go, with Jenny the last of the last, the youngest, arrived in Miami International Airport, arrived at the doorway of God's waiting room, as the old joke had it. Not to die herself, but to help her two oldest sisters die, Eva and Naomi, hovering, endlessly horribly hovering on the brink. Eva was ninety-five, Naomi was ninety, Flora eighty-five, and she, Jenny, was eighty. Neat arrangement, the five-year intervals. "Every five years makes a generation," Gertrude Stein had written somewhere, and was right, at least about these four sisters.

But the immediate job before Jenny was to get herself transported from the airport to the beach. Not easy. Miami was treating Jenny as heartlessly as Jenny was disowning Miami. Though she had clearly told the porter that she needed the SuperShuttle to the beach, he had dropped her and her heavy luggage at the deserted end of a platform where everything was passing her by. She saw herself as if on film—a long shot of a white-haired woman stranded in a chaotic scene of cars, buses, limos, vans, cop cruisers, taxis, motorcycles careening by in a roar of sound, strangely muffled. This old woman who was herself wore a thin black wool suit, a silk knit top visible at the jacket's opening, real pearls glowing against the dark fabric, a mink coat slung over one arm, and covering her only slightly rounded shoulders a cashmere shawl (in case the plane became chilly or a sudden cold spell hit Miami). Her swollen feet were crammed into soft black kid shoes, and the off-black hose were badly wrinkled at the ankle. Nevertheless. No little-old-lady-in-tennis-shoes image for this woman. Elegance, if it killed. It would certainly wound. Her feet would ache for a night and a day.

She must not die in Miami. She would die in New England where she lived. Or in New York City, where Mama and Papa and her three brothers were buried. Actually, the family plot was located in Brooklyn among the massed graves of what Jenny's daughter called cemetery slums. For herself, Jenny didn't really care where she died as long as she was cremated and the urn buried under the white lilac bush behind her studio in Maine.

Forget Miami, forget the family plot in Brooklyn. Concentrate on here and now.

"Aren't we supposed to go out in order, oldest

first?" Naomi on the telephone yesterday morning, begging Jenny to come help her with her dying, though not in plain words naturally, adding an unspoken bargaining plea to Jenny and God that Eva go first. Naomi had cancer. Eva had no diseases but old old age. Jenny herself had no jurisdiction, and it looked as if God was not going to oblige. Naomi was going to die first. Jenny had come, answering her next oldest sister Flora's cry for help as well. "You have to come down, Jenny, I can't do this alone." The four sisters, together, ninety-five, ninety, eighty-five, and eighty. She laughed, this youngest sister of eighty, though there was nothing to laugh about.

So here she was.

She had flown in from Bangor, Maine, and was stifling in her northern costume. The afternoon air was hot, humid, heavy with exhaust. Exhaust. Miami had already exhausted her and she had hardly arrived. There hadn't been a tourist killing in Miami for several months, but she fit the perfect victim profile and would probably revive the trend. She reminded herself that she was, in fact, a minor actor in the New York intellectual scene, she was Somebody, however ridiculously middle-class pretentious Nobody she seemed at the moment. It had been a mistake to aim for elegance. She should have come as Nobody in worn jeans and her brilliantly colored down jacket, made in China. With the mink over her arm, she was tightly clutching a green cloth carryall imprinted with the *Time* magazine logo; nothing could have announced more plainly that her valuables were in the cloth bag. She had placed her larger piece of luggage too close to her feet, and she was in danger of stumbling over it without making a move.

She put her hand on her chest to help her breathing; the air was like hot tea. She waited. Someone or something must come along to help. A cop car skidded past, more like a kiddy-car. Resolutely leaving her luggage unattended, she stepped out into the traffic and waved for help with the arm holding the *Time* carryall. The cop toy went right by, but a second appeared immediately behind it. She waved frantically. The driver was determined to ignore her. She placed herself squarely in his way.

The young cop swung to a stop and inquired in disgust if she was trying to kill herself.

"Right in the line of traffic, lady? Not too smart?"

Apparently a question, but he didn't wait for an answer.

"What're you doing back here, anyway? You coming or going? Know where you're headed?"

"I have a reservation on the SuperShuttle, officer," she said. She'd try good manners, the great placater.

"You belong all the way down there, lady."

"I told the porter and this is where he dropped me. He said the shuttle would pick me up at this spot," and added, to indicate that she wasn't thoroughly addled, "The shuttle to Miami Beach."

She had stepped back onto the platform, close to her luggage. Now the cop's disgust was for the porter. "Asshole," he muttered under his breath, and took off on foot, leaving his kiddy-car behind. At least she hoped "asshole" was for the porter, and that the parked car meant he was coming back. Vehicles roared around it and him, respectful enough of his uniform and his raised hand to keep from killing him. She wouldn't have wanted him to die for her unless that was the only way out.

In a moment he commandeered a shuttle bus, empty except for the driver and another fellow busy with a clipboard. Silent and sullen, they obeyed the cop's orders. The clipboard guy hopped out, loaded her and her luggage in, asked in English with a strong Spanish accent where she was going and if she had a reservation.

She called up her best manner for the cop first. "I can't thank you enough, officer. Thank you so much."

Clipboard mimicked her in Spanish, repeating her words in a faint falsetto. She would pretend she didn't understand Spanish. She gave him the address on Collins Avenue and added, "Yes, I do have a reservation."

"Miami Beach? You should be down the other end, lady. You can't expect a pickup here. We don't do that."

She hated to be called "lady" or "madam" or "ma'am," or by her first name by strangers.

What, then, what in the world would she like to be called?

The cop, back in his kiddy-car, stuck his head out. "You get this nice lady where she's going, you get her to her destination. Understand?"

"Yes yessir sure sure," Clipboard agreed, and once in the bus relieved himself in a long string of Spanish.

Nice lady. Worse, worse. Time to charm the driver and Clipboard. Should she talk to them in Spanish? That might be the last straw. A pushy Jewish old lady talking to Caribbeans in her stilted Castilian Spanish. She chose English.

"I can't thank you enough for your help," she said. "Thank you so much."

"She's a regular Virgin of Cavadonga," Clipboard said in Spanish. The driver laughed. Encouraged, Clipboard mimicked, "Thank you, thank you," in falsetto Spanish again, and then, in his own deep voice, "Enough with the thank yous, please, just permit us to get our fucking job done, thank you, please, thank you."

"*Cuidado,*" the driver said. "She might understand."

"Nothing," Clipboard said. "This kind understands nothing. I have the greatest reverence for old age, you who know me like a brother above all know that I revere the aged, but these old Jewish farts disgust me. They don't know how to grow old, they are totally without dignity. Pushing in ahead of others." He shifted to English. "We're full up on that run, where we going to find the space?"

"All right, okay," the driver responded in English,

switching to Spanish for "Shut up already, you get started you never know when to stop," then back to English. "The lady's got a reservation, check it out."

"Check it out, check it out," Clipboard repeated in despair, and added in Spanish, "I'm lucky if I have time to check out my own shit."

"*Cuidado*," the driver said again. "I can see by her eyes she knows what you're saying."

"What eyes? They don't have eyes. Our women have eyes, even the old ones can kill you with a flash of their eyes. All these old farts have is eyeglasses."

"Jesus," the driver prayed, "shut this guy up, will you, before I go completely crazy."

"Amen," Jenny said, but to herself.

Settled at last in a different air-conditioned bus, comfortable in the high leather seat directly behind the driver, she told herself to pay no further attention to the continuing muddle of the SuperShuttle schedule. She never should have listened to her sister Flora about taking the shuttle. Penny-saving Flora, who certainly had more money than Jenny did. What she wouldn't give to have been met by a limo. She astounded herself by falling asleep for a split second, and was instantly awakened by the sound of her own snorting breath. Another indignity. She never used to snore.

There were apparently only three other riders for Miami Beach: a sloppy teenaged girl backpacking a tremendous load, wearing ripped jeans and a tiny scarlet top ending just above her navel, seemingly sick, yawning violently every few minutes, filling the bus with the nauseating stench of what was probably trench mouth; a very tall blond young man in expensive baggy leisure clothes who placed himself and his pile of soft leather luggage on the farthest back seat to avoid the dirty teenager—and probably to avoid Jenny as well; and a nattily dressed white-haired man who asked permission to sit up front next to the attractive black woman driver and immediately began telling her jokes in Brooklynese.

"A rabbi, a priest, and a dentist went to a bar . . ."

Jenny screened out the rest, and they took off as the driver announced her name to the bus: Angelica.

Angelica screamed with laughter at each punch line, her body heaving, the bus careening. In between the dapper fellow's jokes she inserted intimacies of her married life. Her husband didn't like her to work. He thought she should stay at home taking care of their three children. She disagreed strenuously, as if he were right there in the bus arguing. "Listen, they're not babies anymore, the youngest is seven, they're all in school. They take good care of themselves. I always wanted to drive these shuttles. I'm a good driver, one of the best, but it took time to get me where I am, took plenty of time, lots of hard work, all those lousy runs, now I'm doing it, now I got what I worked so hard for, I'm not giving it up for nobody." More jokes, followed by more intimacies. Angelica loved driving the shuttle, loved people, loved Miami thruways, loved the waterways, loved the heat and the air conditioning, loved talking and listening to her passengers. "It sure beats Chicago," she said. "I don't know why anybody stays in those northern cities." The old gent punctuated her revelations—"Great!" "Good for you!" "You're terrific!" "Attagirl!"—and went on with his next joke. Angelica laughed as the top-heavy bus swung sharply to left and right.

Jenny glanced behind her. The sick girl was asleep, her skinny body rolling about. From his haven in the last row, the handsome young man sprawled pleasantly, legs spread, arms resting on the back of the seat in front of him. Jenny smiled; he responded, rolling his large blue eyes in the direction of the front seat's ongoing skit, fluttering his fingers for the erratic driving style.

Was he gay? Headed for South Beach? An actor? Filmmaker? No. Filmmakers rode in limos. Not only gays rolled their eyes. Her own thoroughly heterosexual son rolled his eyes, also large and blue. Stupid ruminations on her part. No offense. No judgments, just observations.

She forcibly turned her attention to the landscape.

Landscape. No longer a word descriptive of Miami Beach. What had been original to pristine Florida was now entirely paved, restructured, and redesigned. Nature, Darwin, God himself (or herself) had been flummoxed. *Flummoxed.* Nobody said "flummoxed" anymore. Landscape. Seascape. Land and sea, rivers and woods, scrub and sand, flowers and blossoming fruit trees, sharks in the ocean, crocodiles in the swamps, animals and snakes in the jungly matted undergrowth, birds, birds, birds in the strange silvery gray trees, birds, birds, birds strutting, preening, and skittering on the endless stretches of beach, still other birds sheltering in the tall gracefully bending grasses. Once Florida had been an astonishing seascape and landscape. Now it was astonishing, period.

She had expected to hate Miami Beach on her first visit in the late forties, after the Second World War, when Mama and Papa retired to Eighth Street near Washington on their son Max's money. The overnight train trip on the Silver Meteor had been hard. The coach car was jammed. The whole country seemed on the move along with the returning servicemen. Jenny was leaving her first husband, the father of her two children. The children were with her. Guilt made her fuss too much over their four- and two-year-old comfort, their entertainment, their food and sleep. She read to them, sang songs, played games, held them on her lap in turn, settled and resettled them in the uncomfortable coach seats, took them to the unsatisfactory expensive dining car, to the smelly lavatory, to the messy drinking fountain, kept them happy, prayed to God to keep them happy while she went about her selfish business of doing them irreparable harm, tearing up their safe little lives by divorcing their father.

She and the children had left New York in a snowstorm. After an evening, a long night, and a long next day in the crowded car, heavy with the smells of their wintry start, it was astonishing to step out of the debris of the train into hot moist air, burning sun, lush green, vivid vulgar flowering. She had never experienced that sensation before—from harsh winter to instant semitropics.

The children fell in love with Theirami: fabulous wide white sand beach, blue-green violet white-edged water warm and gentle as a bath, palm trees everywhere heavy with coconuts, real coconuts they took home to Grandpa to open and demonstrate how to eat, real coconuts lying around the walkways of Miami Beach like garbage on New York City streets.

Jenny was a city product, born in Brooklyn, reared in every borough except the wilds of Staten Island. Her natural habitat was sidewalks, city parks, museums, public beaches, ferries, a fifth-floor walkup, her father's neighborhood grocery store, the apartment house stoop, public school playgrounds, public libraries, city colleges, corporation offices, bank cages, department stores, five-and-tens, automats. Nature was a brave little blade of grass growing in a chink of pavement, the spire of a building cutting into a sky dramatic with clouds and sunset The height of nature was the open upper deck of a two-tiered Fifth Avenue bus on a soft summer night. Music of the spheres? Beethoven's Pastoral had poured into her, bouncing off the stone benches of Lewisohn Stadium, entrance fee a quarter, or was it fifty cents? She had gleaned the nothing she knew of the natural world then from books, movies, plays. Who dreamt of sharks in Coney Island waters, or snakes, poisonous or otherwise, in any grass of her acquaintance? Did wild animals exist outside the safe borders of the Bronx Zoo?

So what was she talking about anyway? Even now, living in Maine, next door to a wilderness, gathering her half-assed knowledge of trees, plants, and flowers, of barn owls, Canada geese, and pileated woodpeckers, listening to the big noises of the sea and the little noises of life in the woods—field mice and chipmunks, squirrels, voles, ferrets, chickadees, evening grosbeaks, ducks, owls, bats, seagulls and cormorants, foxes and raccoons, skunks and porcupines—and on to the larger animal life, deer, moose, eagles, ospreys, the darling seals, the whales, and the bears, the unbelievable bears. Did this late-gained knowledge give her leave to mourn the natural world of Florida, gone to concrete? When it came down to nature she was a voyeur—and a wimp. She killed any bug that entered her house in Maine, and trapped any mouse. Nature was outside. Her house was inside. Not to be confused. Last year, when she visited her oldest sister, Eva, in posh Aventura, a very large brilliantly green fly had menaced her for most of a morning on the beach, seriously interfering with her reading of Patrick White and necessitating much waving of the arms and flinging about of a towel to keep the insect at bay. And as she swam her labored laps in the chlorinated waters of the condominium's pool, she had been flabbergasted by the visit of a high-stepping heron sipping a drink, its beak alarmingly bleached at the tip.

Flabbergasted, she thought, admiring the effect out her window of a mass of brilliantly white highrises edging the darkened waters on either side of the densely trafficked causeway. Nobody said "flabbergasted" anymore. Something about Miami put time into reverse. Something about returning to the bosom of her family. *Bosom*. Nobody said "bosom" anymore, either.

"A man goes to the rabbi of an Orthodox congregation and asks him to say a *brucha* over his Maserati."

The dapper old gent on a new joke.

Angelica wasn't listening. She was lining up destinations. They had swung onto crowded Collins Avenue, and she was all driver, busy with Miami Beach traffic.

"We'll drop you first, Mr. Winer."

He had become Mr. Winer somewhere along the route when Jenny wasn't listening.

"Then the lady, and then you." Angelica nodded to the young man by way of the rearview mirror. "She's last, way out above Bal Harbour," about the youngster still asleep.

"'What's a Maserati?' the Orthodox rabbi says, so the man goes to the Conservative shul and asks the same question." The joke relentlessly proceeding.

"Fountainblue, right, Mr. Winer?" Angelica pronounced the name of the hotel in pure American, interrupting without apology.

"Right, right, nothing but the best. For me, nothing but the best," and without transition, "and gets the same answer, 'What's a Maserati?' So the man goes to the rabbi of the Reform congregation and tries again. 'Please would you say a *brucha* over my new Maserati?'" Mr. Winer paused to enhance the effect of the punch line. "And the Reform rabbi says to him, 'What's a *brucha*?'"

The blond, blue-eyed, handsome, possibly gay man Jenny had assumed to be non-Jewish joined her in a burst of laughter. Well, well. Jewish after all? Mr. Winer was delighted with the unexpected response from an audience he had long given up on. He turned around to beam at them. Angelica didn't laugh. She either didn't know that *brucha* meant a blessing, didn't appreciate the intricate schisms among the Jewish faithful, or was too preoccupied with rounding the sharp curve on Collins Avenue before the entranceway to the Fontainebleau Hotel.

Directly in front of them, an enormous *trompe l'oeil* Fontainebleau rose over the avenue, a phantom Fontainebleau superimposed on the real one, its gates commanded by pastel-painted Grecian godlike figures guarding the opening to an Eden permanently held within a perfect, unchanging skyscape.

"Ahh!" Jenny said aloud.

Though she had seen this vulgar wonder on earlier visits, it continued to amaze, trip after trip.

"The city made them do it," the young man in the back seat informed her. "To cover up the parking lot, delivery trucks, garbage bins, all the sh—" He checked himself in deference to her white hair. "All the messy stuff, you know. Quite an effect, isn't it?"

Jenny agreed it was quite an effect.

Mr. Winer said, "Gorgeous, gorgeous."

Angelica's strong arms had maneuvered the bus through a snarl of traffic into the crescent beyond the showy fountain and the mass of flowers and greenery. She was all dedicated business inching for a space close to the marbled staircase that led to the hotel's gilded, glowing interior.

Almost all the people pouring out of the mess of vehicles were Orthodox Jews, not the poor European shtetl variety, but new affluent Americans, dressed to the nines, their heads covered. The older women wore fashionable wigs, nothing like the ones Mama's generation stuck on their heads—*sheitels*—and the young women wore charming flower-decorated hats over their glossy wigs. The men covered their hair with little round yarmulkes, silk, embroidered, knitted. "Custom-made" was clearly the rule for their clothing, as was "Money is no object." Whole families were dressed alike, from the mother down to the littlest girl, in long flowered dresses and pretty hats pulled low over luxuriant hair and dark eyes. Often the young mother, leading a brood of four, five, six children, was again proudly pregnant. The tiniest boys wore formal dark suits, the whitest of white shirts, dark ties, and yarmulkes or little fedora hats, like their older brothers and their young fathers. Some of the elderly men were sweltering under traditional long black wool coats and wide-brimmed beaver hats. There were beards, beards, beards and a sprinkling of sidecurls and the dangling strings of snowy white traditional undergarments. It was Passover week. The Orthodox were gathering for the holiday.

Mr. Winer had disembarked, mingling with his fellow Jews and supervising the movement of his luggage. Now that he was safely among his kind, he fixed a yarmulke to the back of his head with a bobby pin as Angelica took off.

Typical of Miami Beach, the neighborhood changed every few blocks. The stretch of Collins where Flora lived was seedy: small old shopping malls, food and drug supermarkets, liquor stores; the usual huddle of worn-out McDonald's Burger King Wendy's Denny's IHP pizza joints Cuban takeout Italian kosher; a collection of hole-in-the-wall stores selling jewelry, T-shirts, bathing suits, shoes, sneakers, lottery tickets, body building and self-defense, eyeglasses, foot care, haircuts, fake nails, psychic readings, tours, money, newspapers, and cruddy groceries. The narrow sidewalks were awash in trash—paper and plastic, food and the debris of its packaging, leaves, sand blown in from the broad beach one block away.

The imposing condominium where Flora had bought an apartment years before stood serene in this general wreckage. Flora got it for a song, as she always said, at a time when the developers hoped the area would boom. But the Rochester Arms remained an isolated bastion on the street, and though the value of the apartments had more than doubled, the surroundings had steadily deteriorated.

Because the driver was not allowed to help with Jenny's bags—"Lady, it's the rule. I can't leave the vehicle unattended"—Handsome jumped out and offered his services. The messy teenager slept on. Jenny paid her eleven-dollar fare, gathered together her smaller bags, coat, and shawl, and followed the young man as quickly as she could. As he hauled her heavy luggage through the littered gardens leading to the door, walking well in advance of her, she noted a cunningly worked embroidered yarmulke pinned to the back of his silky straight blond hair.

Flora had gotten the time of Jenny's arrival wrong. Jenny could hear her shrieks at the other end of the intercom when security called from the desk to say that she was on the way up.

Jenny expected Flora outside the elevator on the sixteenth floor, but the silent, heavily carpeted hallway was empty. She dragged her stuff to Flora's half-open door, decorated with a huge purple paper rose. Flora was hiding behind the door, naked, except for a dark purple towel wound around her head, from which black goo oozed down the pearly pink flesh of her neck into another purple towel draped around her shoulders. The flesh of her body, the well-shaped breasts and legs, denied eighty-five years of wear, but her heavily lined face claimed them.

"It's cigarettes," Eva, the oldest sister, always said. "Flora smoked since she was fifteen—earlier even, she was a devil from the day she was born. She did everything, you name it. Smoking was nothing, you don't know the half of it. It gave her those terrible wrinkles. It's a well-known fact that smoking creates wrinkles. Look at the rest of us—hardly a line on us, not a line. She did it to herself with the smoking. Sure, we all smoked, but not the way Flora smoked. She lived it and breathed it. And now she's paying the price."

Excessive. Flora had always been excessive: the wrinkled skin, the prominent beaked nose dotted with darkened pores, the wonderfully alive black eyes flashing under the heavy black eyebrows. At the moment of greeting she always struck Jenny as an exaggeration of herself, a wicked caricature— particularly now, naked, with the black goo and purple towels. Purple was Flora's color of the decade. In the apartment everything was color-coordinated: light lilac walls, violet and plum for the upholstered furniture, violet again for the cushions and wall-to-wall carpeting, dark and light purple for the throw rugs, the lamps, the window blinds, the pots holding artificial plants, down to the towels, washcloths, bath mats, and purple toilet seats in the two bathrooms. There was even a small upright purple piano.

Jenny embraced, kissed, squealed in response to her sister's welcome, until Flora's joyful noises turned to sobs. Jenny didn't follow down that path.

She had always held herself aloof from the operatic drama of Flora's swings of emotion.

"I can't take it, I can't take it," Flora moaned. "She's dying, Jenny, Naomi's dying. It's too much. Thank God you've come, I can't do this alone. And Eva, she's fading, she's going. It's too much. I can't, I can't. Our sisters are dying, Jenny, they're dying."

"Okay, okay," Jenny soothed. She loved Flora, she did, but this invasion of needy flesh slightly nauseated her, the heaving bare breasts pressing, the oozing goo of the hair dye. Too liquid. She was too dry, too tired. She forced herself to hug and kiss, patting the naked solid female body of her sister, repeating, "Okay, okay, it's okay, Flora. I'm here. We'll do this together."

And wished she were elsewhere.

Flora must have felt Jenny's inner withdrawal, for she in turn withdrew to the farthest of the two purple bathrooms, where she blew her nose loudly and thoroughly. She reappeared in a moment, wearing a wraparound purple terry robe, and struck a pose, arms up, one bare leg extended, laughing immoderately.

"Ta-da! For your eyes only. The one and only Flora at her toilette! No more crying. 'April, April, laugh thy girlish laughter; then, the moment after, weep thy girlish tears.'" And matter-of-factly, "This gunk has to stay on for a few more minutes. Bear with me. I know you don't approve. You don't have to say a word. You go with gray. Fine. I'm dyeing till the day I die." Flora revved herself up into laughter again. "We die a little every day, don't we, *schvester*? Well, while I'm dying, I'm dyeing. I'm living and looking good right up to the minute they put me in my coffin. Think I'm going to go like Eva and Naomi? Not me. I'm dying with my boots on. With my hair black."

Jenny laughed. "You're looking great, Flora." And added, though she knew she shouldn't, "Naomi's hair was still black last time I saw her. Without dyeing. It's extraordinary, isn't it?" And quickly made amends. "You're really looking great."

"What? Even with this?" She pointed at her head. "You weren't supposed to come until I was finished." And then, with a tinge of resentment, "You're the one who's looking great. Weren't you very sick? Gout or something? That's what Eva told me. You know Eva, with her 'poor Jenny' litany. 'Poor Jenny can't even walk, she has such bad gout.' You know Eva, I don't have to tell you."

"My gout's under control. Allopurinol, bless it. I tore a ligament. Fell on a patch of slippery grass. Sheer hell. Most painful thing I ever lived through. Worse than gout."

"You kidding? Worse than childbirth? Nothing worse than labor pains."

"Oh well," Jenny said, "it's all relative."

"It's all relatives!" Flora shrieked. "Sisters, sons, that's all that's left, relatives. You know I haven't got a friend in the world? All gone. Dead. Men, women, friends, lovers, husbands, all gone. Only relatives. My sisters and my sons. My sons can't be bothered and my sisters are dying."

"How is Naomi?" Jenny said. "Is she in a lot of pain?"

"No pain. Don't talk about pain. I don't want you *tsitsering* over Naomi, that won't do her any good. The doctors assure me she's in no pain. Whatever she says."

"What does she say?"

"Listen, she's a complainer. Naomi was always a complainer. A quitter. I'm no quitter, no complainer. I don't want to talk about it. It's not the way I'm going to die. Listen, I have to wash this stuff out now. Nice 'n Easy. Sure, sure. That's what they call it.

It's a mess, but I do it in the shower. I cleaned out a drawer for you and made a little space in the closet. Right here. Settle in. I'll be out in two seconds. If you need hangers, there's a bunch on the closet shelf. I figured you wouldn't have much stuff, only here for a week, right?"

That was wrong, but Jenny said nothing. Time, time, plenty of time to arrange the matter of staying as long as Naomi needed her. Or maybe no time. How long, how long for Naomi, or for Eva, who might go any night, in her sleep if it pleased God or whomever, how long for any of them, Flora or herself, they were all old enough to go. Eighty, eighty-five, ninety, ninety-five. Patients in God's waiting room. *Oh God, let there be time for me to get out of Miami Beach, time to get back to New York or New England.*

Kicking off the shoes that pinched, she padded over the soft purple carpeting of the bedroom to the wide purple-draped windows, drew up the heavy purple shade, and bared the view of glorious seascape. Well, not entirely glorious. The sea side of Collins presented a mix of styles. Street sleaziness had infiltrated its pretensions.

Directly below, the broad deck of the condominium was irreproachably paved, swept, and washed down, properly railed and locked against assailants, its Olympic-size swimming pool filled with clear blue-green water, luminous in the blazing sunlight, its deck chairs plentiful, symmetrically lined up and gaily covered with striped mats that matched the umbrellas opened over occasional round stone tables and benches, its shuffleboard pattern immaculate in matching white and green boxes and stripes, its flowered plantings a mix of rich greenery and the multicolored blossoms of impatiens. There were no living beings on the deck. Wrong time, too hot, height of the afternoon.

Below the broad, high deck the sleaze began. Humanity blossomed—regular-issue, across-the-board humanity. The beach below the condominium was clearly a public one. The wide, wide expanse accommodated crowds of sunbathers—singles, couples, whole picnicking families heavy with kids and paraphernalia: coolers, umbrellas, chairs, beach towels, water skis, water wings, wet suits, beach balls. Bathers came in all colors—gray, pink, white, brown, black. The sand was not the fine white stuff of South Beach but a gritty black-tinted gray. It would have looked uninviting in its natural state. Littered, it was ugly, dotted with large overflowing wastebaskets and messed by the blackened tracks of the garbage trucks. Even the residue of the sea at the shoreline, rocks, stones, shells, carcasses of marine life, formed into an untidy heap on a ridge caused by a steep dip in the ocean floor.

The back of the beach, closer to the terrace, deteriorated even further. The remains of an attempt to beautify left a straggling row of browned vegetation as a line of defense against the sea's relentless wash. There were high wooden staircases for public bathers to cross where the street inter-sected. Underneath the nearest overpass a homeless pair had built a nest: mattress, blankets hung for walls, scattered pillows, piles of plastic bags, a tiny stove, cartons, and a homey clothesline of undergarments, his and hers. There was a public water faucet and open-air shower at the foot of the stairs. Jenny could see a young woman fussing with her wet hair, combing and fluffing before a small mirror placed on an upright carton. Her guy was out in the sun drying his hair, toweling vigorously. They called back and forth to one another, a couple conversing in their apartment, the clear high voice of the young woman yelling something about a car. A car? The homeless had cars?

Possible. There were some beat-up old cars parked against the drooping vegetation, in an area prominently marked No Parking.

And yet. And yet. Beyond the disappointment of the littered beachfront lay the sea, the jaunty vacationland Miami Beach sea, a spread of happiness stretching from the endless deep blue horizon to the waves breaking on its long shore, the water streaked in a greeny-white opalescence tinged with gold and with Flora's beloved purple, like a stage set, an illumination of joyous life. The scene built slowly. In the foreground the shell gatherers, the strollers, the runners and walkers in their costumey beach garb, savoring the good feel of their naked feet on the hard sand of the water's edge. Then the bathers in the shallows, roped-off areas of old people on their unsteady withered legs, deliriously active children in the churning surf, an occasional dog. In the middle distance beyond the greeny-white breakers swam a few of the brave, and some surfers rode the high waves. Beyond that were the pleasure craft, small fishing boats, the racers and gliders in the golden waters, before the deep blue waters were claimed by the huge commercial fishing ships, the tankers, and the enormous cruise liners on the far horizon. A scene of incomparably gorgeous gaiety.

"Fantastic," Jenny said. "Sensational. I forgot how great this view is."

"I hate it," Flora said. She laughed, mouth wide open and head thrown back. She was drying off with still another purple towel. The newly dyed hair gleamed black as shoe polish.

She had been quick. She was dressed, quietly for her, in a rumpled cotton khaki pantsuit with a checked orange shirt, at her throat a huge bandanna in not quite matching orange streaked with clashing colors, and at the ready a little peaked cap in brilliant orange with a matching oversized leather shoulder bag.

"I'm taking you to lunch, I don't care how tired you are. Wendy's has a terrific four ninety-five special that you'll love, everything included. I've got plenty of stuff in the refrigerator, but I don't feel like fussing, and I have to leave time to go over my material for a performance I'm giving in South Beach. You're going to love South Beach. That's where the action is. Anyway, I'm sure you're dying to get out into this wonderful Miami air. You want to change? You should change. Did you unpack? Want help? I hate to be helped, I don't like people in my belongings."

"Yes, yes," Jenny said. "No, no. I was admiring your view. Fantastic. I'll just slip into something and unpack later."

There was no logical explanation for her compliance. She was exhausted; she hated Wendy's; she hated the thick, hot air outside. She wanted to flop into a chair and have a cool drink. Flora was still putting on her cockamamie performances? Not that Jenny had ever seen one. Was she expected to attend? Of course. Flora was in Jenny's life to be obeyed. That's the way it had been, and that's the way it would always be. Flora was bossy and older, and there was the long history dating from their childhood of her ability to frighten Jenny into submission.

"How can you hate it?" Jenny said, waving at the view. "It's such fun."

"Look at it. Always there. Who wants to look at that beauty day after day, night after night, the rosy sunrises, the golden sunsets, worst of all the moon on the water. Not me. Not alone. All that romantic shit. That moon could make you crazy, looking at it all alone. Whatever I'm going through, mental, physical, emotional, there it is, doesn't give a shit about me. And the sea, noisy as hell, always making its sound, if I'm awake or asleep, doesn't give a damn, there it is shrieking away, singing its song. Wait till you hear it in a storm, the wind and the sea, God help the innocent bystander. God help the woman alone. Alone, alone, alone with that damn sea outside the window and the beach and the couples and the families. It's a curse to be alone, a terrible curse. That's how we all end up, isn't it? Look at Naomi. You couldn't be more alone than Naomi. Another way we're cursed. We're long-lived. God help the long-lived woman alone. And still she wants to live. Naomi wants to live, can you imagine? Ninety years old, riddled with cancer, she wants to live."

Jenny could easily imagine. In fact she was as fiercely opposed to any of her sisters dying as they were. Why shouldn't they all live forever?

"Listen, we can't live forever," Flora said.

Jenny was struggling out of her winter suit into a black silk pantsuit, choosing from a group of tops in her opened bag a short-sleeved striped silk. Flora talked on while making up her face at a magnifying mirror framed in purple painted wood. She drew wavering black lines around her wonderfully young eyes, and another wavering black line in the middle of each eyelid, which somehow managed to look good. Then she blackened her graying eyebrows and applied too much too red rouge and too much lipstick. She had beautifully even white teeth, bonded at a cost of thousands of dollars when she was eighty. But the final effect of the makeup job was clownlike.

"Okay, here's the thing. We have to help our sisters die," Flora was saying. "Naomi's dying of cancer. She has to die of something, doesn't she? So it's cancer, the big C. She's lucky. She's ninety years old. Okay, so she had a couple of strokes. She recovered completely. She's got all her marbles. No heart condition, no high blood pressure, no diabetes, no arthritis, no major affliction. Just the big C. It's different with Eva. Eva's dying of old age. Nothing wrong with her but old age. It could take years. She's ninety-five. She could live till a hundred, hanging on, doing nothing. With all her marbles. Intact. We have to help them die."

"Is that what they want? Is that what they told you?"

"No, they want to live. They actually want to live. Can you imagine?" Flora said again.

"To live? Yes, everybody wants to live forever. You too."

"I knew you'd give me a hard time on this," Flora said bitterly. "I knew it. And spare me your philosophy, please. You only bring philosophy in to hurt me anyway."

Jenny muttered, "I'm sorry. I just meant that there's a will to live. In everybody. In our genes."

"What for?" Flora shouted. "Our sisters don't do anything. They eat, they sleep, they complain. That's no life. Naomi's still as vain as ever, worrying about her clothes, running to the dry cleaners every *montag und donshtik*. She's got this thing on her lip, it spouts blood like a faucet, does she do anything about it? No, all she does is run with the blood-stained clothes to the cleaners. All she thinks about is her looks."

"Run?" Jenny said, more or less pulled together in the silk outfit. She claimed the mirror from Flora to comb her hair and put on a little more lipstick.

Flora moved away, struck a pose, clearly impatient. "Hurry up, Jenny, I'm starving. Aren't you starving?" She placed the peaked orange cap at a jaunty angle on her moist jet-black hair.

"Run?" Jenny repeated. She hadn't seen Naomi for a year. "Is she beautiful as ever?"

Jenny wanted Naomi beautiful as ever.

"I don't know about beautiful. What can I tell you, Naomi's Naomi. She's got her own way of doing things, nobody can tell her anything. She doesn't eat right, she's too heavy, her own fault, she can't walk, she won't exercise, she ruined her feet with the wrong shoes. Looks were always what mattered, the pointy shoes, the pointy-toed boots, she ruined her feet, her own fault, nobody to blame but herself. She can't see, she never took proper care of her eyes, she insists she has something called macular degeneration, deterioration of the brain if you ask me, the wrong glasses is all it is, too busy having her hair and her nails done to take care of her health. All she talks about are her bowel movements, she just won't listen about bran, roughage, you have to be constipated the way she eats, never eats a salad which is a crime on their part, the residence, they only serve salad if you ask for it, now is that a crime or not? What kind of a retirement residence doesn't automatically serve salad, and how about their cottage cheese and fruit plate, not a piece of fresh fruit on it, only canned, what does canned fruit do for the digestive system? Nothing, nothing. But you can't talk sense to Naomi. Naomi just won't listen to sensible advice."

They were in the gilded, padded hallway, waiting for the elevator. This flood could only be dammed by a compliment.

"That outfit's terrific, Flora, absolutely terrific," Jenny said.

At last Flora was pleased. "Hey, thanks."

Protocol to be fulfilled, Flora added, "You look pretty good yourself, Jenny." But could not leave it at that. "Though I don't know why you insist on keeping gray hair. It makes you look much older. Of course, I have to think about appearance more than you because of my performances. You've never seen me, have you? I do a terrific one-woman show, little theaters, senior centers. It's gotten raves. This one's at the Hebrew Home for the Aged, right in the heart of South Beach. Where the action is."

They entered the glitzy elevator. A boring, *grimpling* music muttered. Jenny smiled. *Grimpling* had been Mama's word for undistinguished performance.

Jenny hadn't thought of it for ages.

"Remember what Mama called that kind of playing—*grimpling*?" she said.

What Flora had no memory of, Flora insisted had never happened. She eyed Jenny blankly. "What kind of playing? You mean the Muzak? I never pay any attention to the Muzak, and anyway Mama never said that. Now, what were we talking about? Oh yes," and continued with her earlier thought, "but hey, you like gray, gray's fine. To each his own, that's my motto, live and let live. I don't tell anyone how to live, what to do. You like gray, gray it is, but you could look a lot younger, Jenny, believe me, but that's up to you, your choice, your choice, gray's fine if that's what you want."

In the lobby a gathering of the infirm in wheelchairs and the mobile in leisure dress waited for the mailman to finish the distribution. Flora pushed Jenny out the lobby door into the intense heat of the Miami afternoon.

"I'll introduce you later," she said. "Plenty of time later to meet this old crowd," as if she and Jenny were immune to age, were still young.

"What about Naomi and Eva?" Jenny said, driving her body against the hot wind, the gritty air, the debris on the uneven sidewalk under the unrelenting sun. "When will we see them?"

"All in good time," Flora said, taking Jenny's arm and half dragging, half pushing her along. "That's tonight. We haven't gotten up to tonight yet. First we have a date with my adviser."

Flora's description of her adviser had led Jenny to expect a charming charlatan.

"He's wonderful, so calm, so understanding, so gentle, so knowledgeable. You'll love him on sight. He's a world-famous surgeon, brain, I think, or maybe heart or lungs, retired now and entirely dedicated to easing death for the terminally ill. You'll love him." Flora, between bites of the not so awful Wendy's chicken sandwich after all.

But Dr. Maypole proved to be quite solid, the perfect Wasp—Brooks Brothers jacket, striped dress shirt, striped tie, chinos, topsiders—in his early eighties, she had been told, but smooth-faced, younger-seeming, tall, slim, with an inward-leaning manner of listening that was endearing and inspired trust. The creepy part was that he was set up in a Best Western motel room for his consultations. He was businesslike, and when Flora became loquacious and embarrassingly emotional about the doctor's services, he was adept at turning her off.

"Your sister has filled me in on the situation of your two older relatives, their illnesses and impending deaths." He leaned forward reassuringly. "Let me repeat what I told her. Because your dying sisters are still free of hospital supervision, you're in a good position to ease their suffering. I've already explained the procedure to your sister, but perhaps it would be in order to go over it once again. This is what you must do."

A faint, commiserating grimace accompanied the consoling manner that worked so well.

"Set them up in your home as comfortably as possible. Hospital beds can be rented if needed, or wheelchairs. Hire a nurse by all means, and any other help that will ease things for you. The entire procedure should not take much more than a week, ten days at most."

His manner became more brisk, matter-of-fact.

"Essentially what you will be doing is withholding food and water while administering medication to ease the discomfort. There will be, at most, one to two days of discomfort, particularly during liquid deprivation, but bathing the lips with a washcloth or paper napkin dipped in cold water eases that."

Was Dr. Maypole aware of the fiery horror he was kindling?

Flora was crying noisily. The doctor lowered the lids of his pleasant blue eyes for the space of a blink, waved a hand in the slightest gesture of irritation, then leaned toward Jenny.

"You must keep foremost the intent to ease suffering, which is what your sisters are requesting."

Jenny was desperately attempting to maintain one of her public faces, a book-jacket face, perhaps her lecturing face—dinner-party face? Incongruous, inappropriate. What face, then?

"I have explained to your sister that I myself eased the deaths of my beloved mother and my beloved older brother. My mother died in her nineties, my brother was in his early seventies, fatally ill with cancer. It was what they both wished for." He paused. "I understand that your sisters, in their nineties, are of the same mind."

"I don't know," Jenny said. Her voice sounded odd to her, as if someone else in the room had spoken, a stranger, from a lectern possibly. "I haven't talked to them yet."

Dr. Maypole's pleasant pale-blue eyes clouded. "I'm afraid I've misunderstood the situation," he said with the faintest intonation of disapproval. He glanced at Flora.

"I could never do it," Flora said. "Jenny's the one. She's not so emotional. She's colder. And she's not religious. That's why I need her. I could never do it alone. I'll help, but Jenny has to do it, Dr. Maypole, that's why I brought her for this consultation. Tell her exactly how to do it. She can do it. She has that coldness. I'm too emotional."

Flora broke up into weeping again, breathing through wide-open dark-red lips. Dr. Maypole lowered his head. He had all his grayish-brown hair, parted sweetly in a short, neat cut that had been popular in the thirties. He and Naomi would have looked nice dancing together. Jenny concentrated on that image as if it might save her.

She heard herself ask the doctor, in that voice she didn't recognize, who would supply the medication that would soothe.

"We do that," he said, and fumbled through the papers on his desk for a leaflet. "I thought you had been given this material, I thought you would be familiar with—"

"Oh, I forgot," Flora said, "I forgot about that stuff. But she knows all that anyway. She thinks Dr. Kevorkian is okay, don't you, Jenny?"

Flora had stopped crying. She was smiling, actually. "Jenny?" she prompted. And then, nervously, "Jenny, what's the matter with you?"

It would have been impossible for Jenny to explain. She was being transported. Anger was transporting her. She was metamorphosing into a dangerous, alien substance, a column of icy steel that burned white, an icy column of white light, a rod of steel to kill Flora outright, to drive through Flora's flesh at that moment, that instant, and then she would walk away from this scene as if it had never happened.

Jenny forced herself to speak. "I'm sorry, Dr. Maypole. I have to think about all this. I wasn't prepared for this."

"But, but—" Flora, indignant. "You certainly were. We talked about Kevorkian. I thought you understood. You agreed with me. You said you'd do it. I'll help, but I can't do it. You said. You said, Jenny, you as good as promised."

"I don't think I took in what you were actually talking about." Jenny kept her face turned toward

Dr. Maypole. "And Eva. Eva has children—and grandchildren, great-grandchildren. We have no business in such a decision. Her children . . ."

"I understood that these sisters were without family," Dr. Maypole said. "The family must be consulted. You must have their agreement."

Flora said, "No, no, she's mixing everything up. Our sister Naomi doesn't have a soul. Not a soul. No children. Her husband's dead. She has no one but us. Nobody but her loving sisters." Flora was crying again, Flora's noisy, juicy crying.

Dr. Maypole signed off, stood up. "May I suggest that you come back to us when you've resolved the problems? It's not an easy decision, but if I may say so, you must keep your eye on the main thing. The easing of the pain of your loved ones, the easing of this painful passage."

"Thank you." Jenny managed to shake his offered hand, walking out before Flora had finished her effusive farewell speech.

"Isn't he a wonder, isn't he a jewel?" Flora began as they left the motel. Then, "What's the matter with you? The air is so thick with anger I could cut it with a knife."

"If you don't know, I wouldn't know how to tell

you," Jenny muttered. "And please let's not talk for a while. Let's just get to Naomi's place, okay? I'd like to take the boardwalk if it's all right with you."

And they were in the middle of a terrible sisterly fight.

"Oh please, spare me your high-and-mighty good manners, Jenny. You don't want to talk to me, fine, just spare me the fake elegance. I'd like to know what my sin consists of, that's all, but of course if you're on your high horse I know what that means, God knows I've been exposed to it often enough. One thing, though, do you mind telling me how long you're planning to honor me by accepting my hospitality? And another thing, it's *my* boardwalk, I'm the one who lives on the beach, so stop talking as if you invented or discovered the boardwalk."

Jenny heard her own voice, loud and ugly. "Ah, here we go on the let's-throw-Jenny-out-of-the-house routine. What a laugh. *Your* boardwalk. I'll be delighted to leave tonight after I see Eva and Naomi. Short enough stay for you? And might I please have the luxury of silence until then? Could I please just walk along your blasted boardwalk in silence? Please?"

Even as she continued the fight Jenny knew that family quarrels had their own underground momentum and this one would run its inevitable course. Still she injected her own venom, and Flora picked up her cue.

"If you think I don't understand the implication of that comment, you're wrong, Sister Jenny. My blasted boardwalk! I know your sentiments. You're no Jew, and we all know it. No, no, no, I'm not talking about not marrying a Jew, you never were a Jew, you were born a hypocrite and you'll die a hypocrite. It has nothing to do with you didn't marry a Jew and didn't raise your kids Jewish. You're not going to pin that on me. You're a self-hating Jew, that's all. You just can't stand to see my fellow Jews together here on the boardwalk. That's what's eating you. You're an anti-Semite to the bone."

"Damn you, Flora, I'm a Jew and my kids are Jews, even according to your beloved State of Israel. And shut up, I don't want to talk anymore, I just want to walk in silence. You're so crazy I can't even figure out what the subject of this conversation is, I swear."

"I'm crazy? You're the crazy one. 'Subject of this conversation.' You think this is one of your classes?

Don't confuse me with one of your adoring students, sister. I'm onto you. I know you from the day you were born, don't forget that. My beloved State of Israel. There you have it in a nutshell. Anti-Semitic to the core."

Flora was screaming. Jenny was screaming too, but she couldn't hear herself as she heard Flora. Nobody paid much attention. There were a few interested glances from passing couples. Jews yelled at one another, nothing unusual in that. On the upside, Flora had turned her back on Jenny, stalking off rapidly. Jenny could see her orange peaked hat bobbing through the crowd ahead.

Only with members of her family did Jenny become this ugly kid, and particularly with Flora. At age eighty. She despised herself yet let the mood invade her, unable to resist the impulse to be as bad a girl as possible. *In my family I'll stay the outsider until the day I die, so I may as well live up to my reputation.*

She drew in deep breaths of what should have been bracing salt air, but swallowed an impurity of odors—fried shrimp, popcorn, pizza, coffee, beer. She was on a two-mile stretch of boardwalk, a nicely put-together addition to the playground of sand

and water, a walkway actually built of wood boards, with rounded wooden railings, stairways, and little shaded resting places, like toy thatched houses, lined with benches. The sea extended to the horizon on the left, the big hotels rose on the right, foliage and flowers everywhere, the arching blue sky and fakey huge clouds placed just so, all the colors bright and dazzling, a scene suffused with the search for pleasure. Hotels reached out beyond the barriers of their extravagant plantings to pit their pools, their music, their cafes and bars against the lure of ocean swimming and sunbathing. Walkers, bikers, runners, joggers, strollers, and the old infirm sitters on the benches faced the indifferently happy, glowing, multicolored sea dotted with a surface play of boats. In this holiday crowd everyone did indeed seem to be Jewish. The broadest, tallest, blondest, most athletic-looking Aryan male turned his back and inevitably displayed a decorative little yarmulke bobby-pinned to his salon-styled hair.

Intent now on climbing out of the hole she had helped dig for herself, Jenny plunged into the gaiety of the scene. She began a game with herself. Pick out the male most unlikely to be Jewish, check out the back of his head. Yarmulke. Was she glad? Sorry?

Did she give a damn who was or wasn't militantly Jewish? Which blessed Jew would pass Flora's eligibility test? Was pure enough? Including herself?

Including herself. Married a Jew the first time. Had two Jewish children. Married the love of her life the second time, a second-generation American of Spanish-Cuban derivation. Nonreligious, as she was. Had her third child. Also Jewish by Israeli standards, son of a Jewish mother. All three children did seders, did Christmas, did Chanukah. Did it all, loved it all. Why not? The more mixed the better. Mush up everybody in the world, all races, all religions.

What did her sister want of her anyway? What did she want of her sister? Why was she fighting with poor old Flora? Habit of a lifetime. Anguish at being cast as the outcast, Sister Jenny as *Shabbes goy*, the unbelieving lout called in to do the menial work forbidden to the faithful, an unfeeling hunk of ice who could kill her sisters, conscientiously following Dr. Maypole's astonishingly cool prescription. All because she had learned to govern her emotions, because she had worked to earn a Ph.D., because she taught literature and read criticism and wrote reviews and books, all because she had married her

beloved Paul, because she had learned to wear mostly black and to speak in cadences no longer tied to
the Bronx, because she had chosen to live in a wider
world than Flora or Eva or Naomi.

Hitler would not have agreed with Flora's dis-
tinctions, of course, but she was not about to bring
up Hitler, God help her, not in the present setting of
lively Jews happily jogging, strolling, sitting, chatting, laughing on the charming boardwalk under the
sculptured blue-skied white-clouded dome of heav-
en over blessedly sunny Miami Beach.

How did these children of the holocaust breathe
this holiday air while it stuck in her throat? What
magic did they work to dispel memory? Especially
the old. Unthinkable to think of the old and their
memories. And the young, suckled on bitterness.
The pretty young mothers and formal young fathers
steering their broods, the little girls in their expensive custom-made matching gowns and hats and the
little boys in their dark suits and fedoras. And as if
in a Spanish *paseo*, the march of the muscular single
young men and the lovely young women, eyeing one
another, longing to be absorbed into one another
and into the life they had resuscitated with such
energy, and yes, faith. Where did they find faith, of

all impossibilities, *faith*, in this faithless, faithless world.

She breathed deeply. French fries. As if she had actually eaten some, a painful heartburn seized her chest. She fumbled for a Tums in her bag, but the bag dropped from her fingers, scattering change, cosmetics, a comb, her senior citizen card in its little leather case, a pen, and a mess of pills. A clutch of athletic fellows instantly came to her aid, bending to pick up the mix of small things, their yarmulkes ringed in a choreographed effect at her feet, as if in a scene from *Fiddler*. She thanked them.

And then Flora was at her side, Flora in her tacky khaki and orange outfit, tearful, pulling at Jenny's arm.

"Jenny, Jenny, how can we be fighting at such a time? Oh, Jenny, let's not fight, I can't bear it." Her wild black eyes melodramatized the plea.

The truth was that Jenny couldn't bear it either.

"Okay, okay, forget it, let's forget it. The whole thing." Again her voice didn't sound like her own. She was miscast, all around, in this drama not of her making.

Flora said, "You want me to apologize? I apologize, I apologize. Though God alone knows for what. But we have to have peace between us. There's too much we have to do. We have to get through this somehow, Jenny, please, please."

"Yes," Jenny said. "No, no." And then, after another deep breath of hotdog (kosher) sea air, she managed to say, "It's okay, Flora, I'm just upset, give me a couple of minutes, I've got this awful heart-burn, just forget the whole thing, I can't do it, we'll work something else out, okay?"

"Oh, thank God, thank God we're not arguing anymore. There are other ways. The hospice people are wonderful, someone told me. We could look into hospice." Flora once again energetically in charge.

"Yes," Jenny said. "In a minute. Right now I need a couple of Tums."

"You need something a lot stronger than Tums," Flora said. "Your doctor is giving you Tums? Have you tried Xanac? Maybe you need to see another doctor. Or is it Xanax? I'm always mixing those two up."

"In a minute," Jenny said. "I'll be all right in a minute."

And pleaded in silence for no more talk.

2
TROMPE L'OEIL

Naomi's residence was close to the Fontainebleau. It had been built in the twenties, and became a gathering place for jazz musicians. A little of that period remained in the splendid glass-splintered chandelier of the lobby. Otherwise it was seedy, though the broad terrace overlooking the wide beach and the sea sported a decorative circular bar under a palm-thatched roof. Nearby was a pitifully tiny mango-shaped pool in which three swimmers would have been a crowd. No danger. One resident in her eighties paddled around at the shallow end every morning before breakfast in a ruffled flowered suit and water wings. And a misshapen skinny man of indeterminate old old age swam an astonishingly perfect crawl every afternoon before dinner.

"Show-offs," was Naomi's dismissive judgment. "Ridiculous show-offs." She also didn't like the fact that the woman who swam dared to wear red high-heeled shoes when she dressed for dinner. She certainly skittered around the dining-room floor dangerously, but then, it was a tiled floor.

Naomi was still pretty, in spite of ninety years, in spite of cancer of the breast metastasized and spreading throughout her body. She was elegantly costumed, in a full skirt mixing flower patterns with bold geometrics that should have clashed but didn't because of the rich meld of colors, a white satin blouse with a cunningly crossed collar that sheltered her ruined neck, and a silk jacket that picked up on the vibrant subtleties of the skirt. Her hair was still black, cut short in a twenties kind of bob (to match the twenties kind of residence?). Her brows were naturally black too, and beautifully arched, without the crazy outcroppings many old people sprout. With the late afternoon sun directly on her pale face, her hazel eyes shone almost clear green. She wore little makeup, a bit of face powder and a light lipstick where the offending spot, which according to Flora periodically spouted blood, showed slightly darker on the upper lip of her charming mouth. Her happiness at Jenny's arrival was pure and childlike. She reached up from her wheelchair and pulled Jenny's face close to hers.

"My baby sister," Naomi said, and kissed her. Her breath held a faint sour odor that Jenny forced herself to meet smilingly. "Do you remember," Naomi went on, caressing Jenny's hair, "do you remember how I always gave you shampoos when you were little? Do you remember? When poor Mama was so busy helping Papa in the store she had no time for you?" She rested her cheek against Jenny's in a silence filled with shared losses.

Jenny stroked her sister's smooth, rounded brow, noble under the silky hair swept away from the innocent part. The sweet parting of the hairs of their heads, Dr. Maypole's and Naomi's. Jenny was supposed to kill this darling sister?

Suddenly Naomi pulled away to vent her annoyance that Flora was off talking to the other residents. "She acts like a social worker. So false. What does she do for them? Nothing. It's all talk. Anyway, she's here to see *me*. Why is she talking to *them*?"

It would serve no purpose to point out to Naomi that it was she who had introduced her sisters to almost everybody in the residence, down to the busboys in the dining room. What was there to do then but be polite and make conversation?

As if she had read Jenny's mind, Naomi said,

"Why shouldn't I introduce you? I'm proud of you. I'm proud of my sisters. Who wouldn't be? I want to show you off. Especially you, Jenny. I was telling this man who recently moved in that you wrote for the *New York Review of Books*. He's a retired professor of philosophy, something like that, and he was very much impressed." She paused. "Though if the truth be told, he's an idiot. Underneath those degrees he's nothing but an idiot. Never heard of *Eugene Onegin*. Would you believe it? By Tchaikovsky, I tell him. Beautiful, ravishing. Never heard of *Onegin*. Idiot. He's crazy about me, but I just brush him off. Please, control yourself, I tell him, and he calms down."

What the retired professor of philosophy heard during conversations was anybody's guess. A neat little man, ninety-seven and still handsome in a dashing Russian-Jewish mold, smelling of talcum and aftershave, well groomed in carefully color-matched outfits—cotton slacks, jacket, tie, dress shirt, fresh flower in the lapel—he was indeed crazy about Naomi, kissing her hand in greeting and leave-taking, but he was so deaf any kind of progressive communication was impossible. He smiled and nodded, nodded and smiled, and once in a while shouted an unhinged response into a disconnected void.

"If a man isn't handsome I can't look at him," Naomi informed Jenny, as she often had in the past. "Or if he smells bad. They have to smell nice. My husband was beautiful and he smelled beautiful. Of course, Shimon isn't that beautiful, but don't you think he looks like John Gilbert, sort of that type? Sam was more the Ramon Navarro type."

Naomi's husband, dead for fourteen years, had indeed been a handsome man even into his late nineties. And yes, if one squinted, Shimon, the retired professor, did look a bit like John Gilbert.

"Poor squeaky-voiced John Gilbert. Couldn't survive the talkies," Jenny said.

"What?" Naomi said, and continued as if Jenny hadn't spoken. "We all had handsome husbands. Except Flora. But Flora has no taste. Especially in men. All they have to be is men, in pants, and in her estimation they're great, as long as they fill their pants, if you know what I mean." She lowered her voice. "Flora told me you two had a fight and you're leaving."

For a split second Jenny caught Naomi's deep-set hazel eyes suffused with suffering and unspoken longing before their sculpted lids hid the emotion.

"Please don't go, Jenny. I'm so frightened. Another operation. You know I have to have another operation. This time in my—you know, near the groin. With the one on my shin not even healed yet. And I had two, you know, on my breasts. One on each breast. But of course you know, you came to be with me. Bless you, darling, bless you for that, but please don't leave me before the operation. Stay with me again." She had delivered this speech to her own lap, never looking at Jenny after the first agonized glance. And without transition, holding her mouth rigid, she said, "Why can't I just die quietly, smiling, why can't I just die in my sleep or sitting in a chair, why must I be so tormented and make the people around me suffer? I wanted to go out smiling, not this big bother to everybody. Is that too much to ask?"

Jenny leaned over to hug her. "No, no, you're not, I love you, I'm not leaving. No, no, yes, of course I'm staying."

Naomi looked up. "I'm sorry, Jenny, I don't have the strength anymore. I can't. Who's right, who's wrong. I just want peace around me. Forgive me, but I can't. I can't take sides, I need whatever help I can get, I need her. I need Flora, I need you, whoever's right, whoever's wrong. It's too late for right or wrong, right or wrong is too hard for me now."

"It's okay," Jenny said. "I'm not leaving Miami. I'll be here, don't worry. You're right, it doesn't matter. I'll be with you, I promise."

She had never before considered the phrase "Her heart sank." It wasn't her kind of phrase, but it was happening to her at this moment standing beside Naomi's wheelchair, her heart sinking through her body down down into her trembling thighs and legs and feet, down through the dreary green carpet of the chandeliered 1920s lobby in the run-down residence, her heart sinking slowly heavily yearningly beneath the floor through the cement foundation through the pipes and messy obstructions to the earth, the real earth that her heart longed to be buried in, never to rise to feel more loss.

Flora was slowly approaching with a companion pushing a walker, a woman all roundnesses: smiling face, red fluffy hair, bosom and buttocks under soft blue clinging pantsuit. Lift, push, drag, step. Lift, push, drag, step. They inched forward.

"Dolly's son gets the *New York Review of Books*," Flora threw out in advance of their progress. "She's dying to meet you, Jenny."

Dolly's son was apparently one of those forever

graduate students, in his late thirties, working on his thesis. Dolly said he regularly read the *New York Review of Books* but on second thought perhaps it was the *New Yorker*, she might be mixing them up.

"That's okay. Jenny's written for both." Flora, filled with pride. "She's a published writer, books too, you know."

It was a toss-up for Jenny which was worse, Flora's intimate scorn or Flora's public praise filled with errors. She had never written for the *New York Review of Books*.

"The *Women's Review of* . . ." Jenny stopped herself.

Dolly, reluctant to abandon the topic of her graduate student son, who was, it appeared, also writing a book, asked if it cost Jenny a lot to get her books published.

"No," Jenny said. "They pay me, not a great deal, but I don't pay them."

"I have a cousin," Dolly said, leaning her round bosom against the front of the three-sided walker and returning the smile to her round face, "a very educated man, he paid to have a book published. They turned out a beautiful job, all in blue with a little red trim."

Naomi threw back her head and closed her eyes.

"Why haven't they opened the dining room? I'm starving."

Dolly turned to Naomi. "You have to be patient. It doesn't open until four o'clock on the dot, not a minute earlier. They're having fish tonight. I don't like their fish, but what can you do?"

"Dinner's served at four o'clock? I thought it was five," Flora said.

"I changed my seating," Naomi said. "Took the earliest seating. I couldn't wait."

"You have to learn to be patient." Dolly inched her walker to the side of Naomi's wheelchair. "How many times have I told you, Naomi darling, you have to be patient. Your sister is a wonderful person, but she has to learn to be patient." The last directed to Flora and Jenny.

"Too many," Naomi said, her eyes closed, "too many times. Anyway, it's late for patience. Patience is for the young to learn." She searched through her carryall to find a brimmed cotton hat that she pulled down over her forehead, an enchanting addition to her outfit. "No more talk. It's too exhausting." And under her breath, "Too boring."

"Are you cold?" Jenny asked. "Shall I get your shawl?"

"No, the light hurts my eyes."

"Sunglasses," Flora said. "Why do you insist on not wearing your sunglasses?"

"I like hats better. Hats cut the light. And they're pretty."

"*And* sunglasses," Flora emphasized. "I wear both."

"You go out in the noonday sun with the mad dogs and Englishmen," Naomi said. "I stay out of the sun."

"The sun's good for you," Flora shot back. "And please spare me your so-called wit. The sun would do you good."

"So you say." Naomi pulled her hat down lower and muttered, "Welcome to our jolly gathering of the lame, the halt, and the blind."

The lobby had jerkily filled with the oldest and most infirm of the residents waiting for the doors to open on the first seating of the evening meal. A few walked on their own, but most relied on canes, walkers, wheelchairs, or one another for help. They were predominantly women, made up, hair done, nails polished, narrow slacks straining over big bottoms, fancy tops, embroidered, sequinned, hand-painted, printed, tight across full slack bosoms and dowager humps. Some of the few men present wore jackets, dress shirts, ties; some were in incongruously snappy leisure suits.

Under cover of the movement into the dining room Naomi whispered, "Jenny, could you come alone tomorrow morning? There's something I have to tell you. I don't want Flora to know."

Naturally, there had to be a touch of family intrigue. And intrigued Jenny was. "Of course. First thing in the morning. Nine o'clock too early?"

"I don't want Flora to know. You call nine o'clock early? I'm up every morning at five."

"Okay, I'll manage. Nine o'clock. Alone."

"Wheel me in," Naomi said aloud, "with the rest of the deaf and the dumb dumb dummies, dear sisters," and laughed. "I'm paying for your dinners. Eight fifty apiece, and please don't forget or they'll try to get you to pay again. Just tell them your sister put you on her bill."

"Do we tip?" Jenny had forgotten from previous visits. "Let me do the tip."

"No tipping." Flora, adamant. "I bring little gifts now and then to show appreciation for how nice they are to Naomi. Tipping spoils them."

"Nice? Why do they have to be nice? I don't

give them any trouble. There's no need for little gifts. Nice!" Naomi, indignant.

"I like to show appreciation," Flora said. "In the end it pays. People like to be appreciated. In the end they do more for you."

"The less they do for me the more I like it," Naomi said, and recited parts of the menu as they wheeled her past the blackboard. "Pea soup. Good. I love pea soup, but not the croutons. Too hard on the teeth. I hope they skipped the croutons. Ice cream. I hope it's butter pecan or rum raisin, but probably no such luck, just dumb vanilla is what we mostly get. They think we don't know any better.

"We *are* in luck," Naomi went on, laughing again. They were passing a baby grand piano on the way to Naomi's table. "I forgot tonight was Wednesday. Miss Molly and Her Songs of Yesteryear. You're in for it. Thank God our table is sufficiently removed."

Miss Molly was a very large, violently redheaded woman in an elaborately beribboned dress. She sat at the piano, *grimpling*. No other word for it. The vamp of an old pop song was being performed with many flourishes and more errors, the verse sung in a quavering off-key soprano. " 'Be sure it's true when you say I love you . . .' "

64

"Forgive her, sisters, she knows not what . . .," Naomi began, but her laughter stopped her.

"She's doing the best she can," Flora said. "She's trying. That's better than giving up. You can't understand the strain of performance. Not that I'd compare what she's doing to what I do."

"Well, we can't all live up to your standards, Flora." Naomi was signaling mysteriously to Jenny. "I give up," she said. "And it's a far, far better thing I do than Fatso there. Time to know when to quit. I quit."

"That's the trouble with Naomi," Flora complained to Jenny under the applause. "She's given up, she's given up."

Wasn't that what Flora wanted Naomi to do?

Jenny, helping settle Naomi's wheelchair at the table, was startled by a pull on her arm and Naomi's hurried whisper.

"Never mind about tomorrow. I changed my mind. I don't want to tell you. Forget about it." She pushed Jenny away. "That's fine. Stop fussing. Now let's eat."

Flora insisted on taking a bus to Eva's residence. They had finished dinner and seen Naomi off to her bedroom, though it was not yet six o'clock. The air in the vehicle was too cold. Flora fished out of her orange leather carryall a brown corduroy outer jacket, an orange knitted scarf, and orange gloves.

"I'm always prepared for these buses. You can get pneumonia in a minute from the air conditioning. Aren't you freezing? I told you to bring something warm."

"I'm fine," Jenny said. "I'm used to the cold."

"I don't know how you stand it up there in that freezing snow and ice, all alone." Then, more cheerfully, "But everybody's different. Live and let live, that's my motto. I'd get pneumonia the first week. Or die of boredom the second, whichever came first." Flora let out her loud, clear laugh.

Jenny coughed.

"See? See?" Flora, triumphant. "I told you."

"It's the air conditioning," Jenny said. "It bothers me, something about it makes me choke."

"I told you, I told you."

"Not because it's cold. It catches in my throat, I don't know why."

"You have to bring something warm to put over your shoulders in the buses. You have to, I told you. Here." Flora dug her arm into the big bag. "I have another scarf in here somewhere." She dragged out a white crocheted shawl and draped it around Jenny.

It was a long ride. Again they traveled through quickly changing scenes and neighborhoods. The bus was filled with Miami Beach workers heading home. The blacks were mostly Haitians; the Latinos were white and black; the white whites were like Flora and Jenny, middle-class oldsters on their way to the movies, or to upscale Bal Harbour shopping and dining, or on a hospital or nursing home visit. Most of them dismounted at Bal Harbour, a short trip from Naomi's residence. The bus had already carried them through remarkably diverse areas, posh, seedy, lush green, arid construction sites, messy concrete disrepair, then over a pristinely beautiful waterway, past an enclosed, guarded state park skirting the beach, and through Flora's run-down neighborhood.

The only people boarding now were workers, Haitians, Cubans. What had happened to Florida's homegrown blacks? Apart from a bunch of noisy teenagers, some of whom were Latinos, there seemed to be no American blacks on the bus. The black driver was carrying on a lively conversation with a woman in the front seat, in Spanish, about a mutual cousin. They had nothing good to say of her. There were some babies, mostly quiet, one crying, and a boy and girl of four or five singing commercials at the top of their tuneless voices, standing backwards on a forward-facing double seat and drumming on the seat back with what seemed to be Ping-Pong paddles.

"What I can't stand about them is how noisy they are—Cubans, or whatever they are." Flora, in loud voice. "And they never discipline their kids. No matter what their kids are up to, they let them get away with murder. Then they wonder why they turn out the way they do."

"Sh!" Jenny said, too late.

Without turning her head or looking in Flora's direction, a middle-aged woman said in Spanish to the young woman next to her, "Listen to Big Nose over there. That Jew is calling us noisy? Did she ever listen to herself? Do they hear themselves? Never. The Chosen People. Perfection incarnate. But please notice the way she's dressed. Beautiful, no? Right out of the garbage, the whole wrinkled mess. She ought to be ashamed of herself. Old lady dressed like a sloppy teenager." She said "mess" and "sloppy teenager" in an almost unaccented English. "Look who dares to speak badly of our children. The way they've raised theirs, raised them to squeeze the life out of others. Hitler should have finished . . ."

"No," the young woman interrupted, also in Spanish. "That kind of talk isn't right. Don't talk that talk."

"You defend them?" the first woman said.

"I defend decency. That kind of talk is bad. There are plenty of fine Jews, and we know it. We all know it. I work for a very fine Jewish lady—"

"Sure. Who buys you with worthless little—"

"Off, off the bus!" The driver, directing the teenage group. "Your stop, and thank God for that."

"I'll say one thing for them," Flora continued blithely. "They're hard workers, they know how to work. They'll do anything. Pay them and they work. And always smiling. Nobody works harder than the Cubans. They put the blacks to shame. But the noise level! God help us."

"Shhh!" Jenny said. "They speak English, you know."

"Oh, very few do. Anyway, I'm complimenting them." Flora put her head back. "I'm exhausted. Could we not talk for a while? I can't stand any more talk right now, if you don't mind." And closed her eyes, pulling the peaked cap down over her face. "If I fall asleep, keep an eye on my bag. You never know." She was gripping the clasp of her carryall with both hands.

They stopped at one of the old street malls. The bus almost emptied, and refilled with similar people, more of these white. Hospital and nursing home workers—nurse's aides, cleaning women, maintenance men, shleppers, drivers, kitchen help—cogs in Florida's billion-dollar industry.

Flora said, without opening her eyes, "I told the bus driver to let us know when we reached Villa Rosa. Listen for it, Jenny, or we'll get lost. You can get terribly lost in Miami."

"It's okay," Jenny said. "I know the cross street, I'll watch for it."

"No, listen for the bus driver. If we go past the stop we'll get terribly lost."

"Yes, I will, I will. Don't worry, go back to sleep."

"Who can sleep with all this noise?" Flora said.

Jenny looked at her sister. Eighty-five, strangling in unfulfillment, dying not to die before accomplishing some vague greatness for which she would be remembered forever, venting prejudices so she could feel herself larger, more vividly significant.

Scared. Scared of getting lost in Miami. As if cabs didn't exist. Scared of spending the money she had in good enough quantity to live out her days in comfort. Scared she would catch a cold. Scared her bag would be snatched out of her lap. Scared she'd fall. Scared she'd break a hip. Scared she'd die. Scared she wouldn't, but would live on and on through a cycle of horrors: cane, walker, wheelchair, bed, pain and doctors, indignity after indignity, alert and resistant all the way to the coffin.

Jenny reached over to tuck the orange scarf more securely around Flora's neck.

Flora snuggled in. "Thanks," she whispered. "Take a nap too. Put your head on my shoulder." Then corrected herself. "Though I guess one of us should stay up and listen for our stop."

"I'm not sleepy," Jenny said. "I'll listen."

They were on a causeway crossing a stunning stretch of brilliant blue water, its edges lined with smallish homes, little docks, little boats. An unidentifiable flock of white birds lifted into the golden evening sky from a small island so green it shone black in this light. Artificial? The island? The waterway? Did it make any difference if it was man-made? Was it less beautiful?

Naomi's request shot into her head, followed by the quick, odd retraction. What was that about? Money. Something about money. What else could it be? Money and Naomi and Flora—had to be some such configuration. Naomi had cautioned her not to tell Flora. A family mess about money. In short, a nightmare.

Now they were stopped at a railroad crossing in another sudden change in the landscape, a neighborhood of little factories, seedy stores, strange characters lounging around in the heat on the sidewalks. The train lumbered by endlessly. A skinny white man sitting directly across from Jenny and Flora muttered crazily.

"Goddamn, goddamn, they don't give a goddamn. Don't care how they treat us. Don't care how late they make us. Time belongs to them. They got everything else, and now they got jurisdiction over time. My time."

He looked desperately unhealthy, unwashed, uncombed, as if he had never eaten right in his life, never slept in a wide clean bed, never taken a long luxurious bath with good soap, never washed his thin greasy hair. His cotton slacks and shirt hung

on a frame without substance. *Coat upon a stick.*
Probably bound for the dog races to lose the last
penny he had in his grimy pocket. Jai alai, maybe.
He quieted as soon as they were moving again.

She thought, *I must go to the bank tomorrow and
check on Naomi's accounts before I ask her what this is
all about.*

The scene had altered once more. They were in
an enclave of high-rise condominiums surrounded
by waterways, golf links, tennis courts, swimming
pools, tree-lined bicycle paths and walks, lush
greenery and flowering plants, pretty as a picture. In
the distance the huge white arches of a thruway
overpass cut into a sky now magnificently stained
with the setting sun. Orange, purple, green. Gaudy.
Gaudy as Flora.

Brave, extravagant, gaudy, foolish Flora. Her
closest sister in age. Her pal, her rival, her self. *There
but for the grace of God.*

Then Naomi, ten years older, a sister-mother,
watching over little girl Jenny, combing and washing Jenny's hair. Delicate, witty, heartbroken Naomi,
longing for someone to watch over her, pouring out
on Jenny the care she craved for herself.

And Eva, fifteen years older, a mother-sister from the beginning, generous, dependable, loving, hopelessly bourgeois Eva.

And herself? Little girl Jenny? Born last to a mother and father too old and worn. Mothered by her older sisters. Bullied, bossed, and petted by her older brothers. Grown into the disguise of a civilized, self-contained intellectual, Jane Witter, academic, essayist, critic.

Nobody ever heard of you, Jenny, except a couple of your New York women friends. Jane Witter, professor of literature, book reviewer, freelance writer of an occasional article. Not even your true name. Witter—borrowed from a Brooklyn apartment house, the Witter Arms. Jenny Witkovsky masked as Jane Witter. You are of a piece with your sisters. A poor thing. Coat upon a stick. Stop disowning them. They are you.

Suddenly the driver called out their stop. They disembarked hastily and crossed a broad avenue heavy with traffic, Flora hanging on Jenny unsteadily, swaying, pushing.

"I feel horrible," Flora said. "I need a drink. I hope to God Eva has some vodka in her apartment."

"She always does," Jenny said.

They entered through tall wrought-iron gates,

past a handsome stone plaque announcing "Villa Rosa." Eva and a black attendant waited just inside the complex. She was in a wheelchair under the shade of a few limp trees planted on the edge of a paved parking lot. Jenny knew it was Eva by her voice; otherwise she was unrecognizable. Her normally narrow, intelligent face had been transformed into the balloon of an idiot. Her skin was covered by a fine gray fuzz along her chin and cheeks. Her dark, large eyes had become animal slits. She was agitated, crying out in delight mixed with incomprehensible rage.

"Jenny, Jenny, I thought I'd never see you again."

This woman Jenny didn't recognize, except for her voice, cried like a child, grabbing at Jenny in a hungry, sloppy embrace, reaching up pitifully with wasted bare arms. How could the face be so round and the arms so thin? Jenny kissed this stranger, her eyes watering, but her tears were for the serene, composed sister she remembered, Eva of the strong slim body and the quick responsive face, who had always been fully in charge of herself and of others. Jenny had never seen Eva cry.

"Eva, for God's sake, what are you doing out without a jacket?" Flora, in her hectoring manner.

"You need to protect yourself from this hot sun." She dismissed the attendant with a brisk "Thank you, we'll take care of her now."

The black man handed over a cotton jacket, a small shopping bag, and a large plastic bag of heavy stuff.

"What is all this?" Jenny said.

"She likes to take her things with her." He spoke with a West Indian accent. "The women take much with them all the time. They like that." He had a wonderfully large white-toothed smile. "No harm done." He leaned over Eva affectionately. "Poor girl has had a hard day, but now she happy. Goodbye, Eva darling, have a wonderful time with your sisters. Take care now," and sprinted out of the heat into the cool building.

"Charles is very angry with you," Eva blubbered. "Because you were so late. I've been waiting for you all day. I've had a horrible, horrible day, Jenny, I didn't know what happened to you after you came here this morning and said you were walking to Jenny's, I mean Flora's. Jenny, why did you walk to Flora's, or Naomi's, or wherever you went with all those thruways and traffic, you could have been killed, what's wrong with you, and with all your luggage. You could have left your luggage with me, I never stole from you yet, I never thought you could be so foolish, I begged you to stay with me."

Flora said, "What are you talking about, what in the world are you talking about? What is she talking about?"

Jenny was ready to say anything to calm Eva. "I'm sorry, darling, I'm sorry I upset you. I thought you knew we weren't coming until tonight."

"Of course she knew we weren't coming until tonight," Flora said. "I spoke to you myself, Eva. After supper, I told you plainly—Jenny and I are coming after supper, after we see Naomi."

"But why did you visit me this morning, Jenny, and tell me you were going to walk to Flora's? Or Naomi's?" She broke into bitter weeping. "And you were so cold and mean, so unlike yourself. With all that traffic on the thruways, Jenny, I thought you'd be killed, I thought I'd never see you again."

"What's the matter with her?" Jenny whispered to Flora during the long tirade. "What have they put her on that she looks this way? She must have dreamt all that stuff, or she's hallucinating. Is anybody checking her medication?"

She didn't say, *This is unbearable. I want my sis-*

ter Eva back, I don't want this mad stranger.

"Her kids aren't paying enough attention," Flora whispered.

"Do they know? Shouldn't we let them know?"

"Listen, I don't interfere. Live and let live. Their business is their business. I don't mix into other people's family business."

"But she *is* our family. She's our sister. And they're wonderful kids. Maybe they don't know, they all live so far away, maybe they have no idea. She sounds fine on the telephone."

"You're not listening to me, Jenny." Eva pulled at her. "You have to promise me, promise me."

The unrecognizable woman was slowly taking on some resemblance to the sister Jenny knew. Underneath the moon face, the hair, and the squinty eyes, Eva was emerging.

"I am, I will," Jenny said, and burst into tears. "I promise. I'm sorry we worried you, I'm sorry, I'll never do it again."

"Am I going crazy, or what?" Flora said, and turned her full attention to Eva. "Now calm down, Eva. Jenny wasn't on the thruway. Jenny wasn't here this morning. We aren't late. We came exactly when we said we would. Nobody was walking on the thruway—"

In the normal voice Jenny remembered, Eva said, "Don't you tell me to calm down, little sister. Keep in mind that I was diapering you before you could say Mama." And turning once again to Jenny, she beckoned in a wide embrace and Jenny was in the arms of the Eva she loved, sane, accepting, generous Eva.

"Oh, Jenny darling, it's so wonderful to see you, so wonderful of you to come. I can't believe it's really you."

"Well, am I *de trop* or something around here?" Flora, sulky. "Shall I make myself scarce? Would you two like to be alone?"

But Flora's sisters weren't listening to her.

Jenny seized on the fleeting argument with Flora to check into a run-down place a few blocks north of Flora's condominium. She was lucky. A couple had unexpectedly moved out of an efficiency apartment on the second floor overlooking the ocean. One room, big bed, a couch, an armchair, all in matching dim stripes, a mongrel bedside piece, a dresser, a table and two chairs, a kitchen, so to speak, a little foyer, then a bathroom. Terrible lighting, some overhead, some lamps. Two doors: entrance from an inner court balcony with a view of some dismal shrubbery, two small, odd-shaped swimming pools, and a funky bar-restaurant with a couple of indoor and outdoor tables; the other door out to a tiny balcony that gave on the sea, a compensation so large it made the rest acceptable.

She was exhausted. She collapsed on a deck chair, wrapped in the moist hot wind, in the mystery of dark heaving water and the whiteness of the breaking waves on the shoreline. She fell into one of those quick naps peculiar to the old and awoke to painful discomfort and a wild disorientation. Where in the world was she?

In Theirami. She was up to her neck in Theirami. That came clear to her after a few moments. She got up, left the sea behind her, drew the blinds against the courtyard lights, turned off the air conditioning, and opened a window. She unpacked. She hadn't unpacked at Flora's. She turned away from the reality of their swift quarrel. Of course Flora would have made up, but Jenny had held tight to the quarrel, using it as an excuse to come to this seedy refuge to be alone. No sin. No harm done. She forgave herself. Take a lesson from Charles forgiving the dotty old ladies for carrying their belongings around with them.

She set her traveling clock on the night-stand/bookcase/desk next to her bed. It was only eight-thirty. She turned on the TV, surfed until she found a *Seinfeld* repeat. Just what the doctor ordered. She watched and laughed, and laughed again. Then laughed at herself unpacking her green carryall. Medications. CDs. All her good jewelry. As dotty as the rest of them. Why hadn't she left her jewelry home? And the CDs? Not safe. Or in her bank deposit box? Too much trouble. Easier to carry them around. Dotty old woman.

Good thing she hadn't undressed, because she should put the jewelry in the office safe. Where it would be safe? One had to believe in something.

The room was now too hot. She closed the window and turned the air back on before she went out. The office-lounge was spooky quiet, with only one dour man in charge, but the patio was lively: very loud rock from the bar; a bunch of German-speaking kids in the bigger swimming pool, in the care of a large male tossing them around in the water like beach balls; at the tables, foreign tourists, down-at-heel locals, one Middle American tourist couple, a handsome Latino sitting alone talking into a cellular phone. There was no sign of Miami Beach's affluent Jewish crowd.

The two-man restaurant staff was straight out of central casting: the waiter fat, the cook skinny; the cook hairless, the waiter nothing but hair, head, face, chest, legs, and arms; the cook totally silent, the waiter garrulous, about himself, where he came from, where he hoped to be going, the food (which smelled unexpectedly good), the weather, the state of the sea, the full moon that had come shining up out of nowhere. Cook and waiter were both half naked to stand the kitchen heat: shorts, sort of underwear vests wet-sticking to the skin, the waiter's long hair in a ponytail tied with a long red ribbon, the cook's bald head partially bound in what looked like a used handkerchief.

Jenny inquired politely of the lone Latino if she might sit with him. He inclined his head in a yes, never leaving off the phone conversation. From the friendly, talkative, fat, hairy waiter she ordered a salad called Tropic Fantasy. It cost $6.35, and when it came was quite beautiful and deliciously fresh, fruits and nuts on a bed of mixed greens.

The Latino put through call after call, some in English, some in Spanish, about a deal so complicated she could not follow in either language. He was Cuban, dropping vowels and consonants freely in both languages. "Nahyea," he kept cautioning. "Don tell noboda. Nahyea." *Not yet*, probably. As she was finishing her salad, a deeply tanned blond American young woman in a dress that barely covered her slim, bosomy torso joined the Cuban. She had an infant on her flat hip, a little girl as dark as her father. Lovingly, he took the child on his lap while repeating the message, "Don tell noboda. Nahyea." He must have made twenty such calls before Jenny settled her bill and left.

The bed surprised. It was comfortable. She kept the windows closed and the air on, trading one discomfort for another. It was a hot night. Heat made her horny. Cold made her horny. Memory made her horny. Music made her horny. Eighty-year-old women weren't supposed to feel horny. They were supposed to be serene, wise, resigned. But here she was, raging in bed, for love, for lost love. At eighty. Grieving. For the loss of her husband of forty years.

Nobody believed in that. One love. The love of one's life. She felt a fool talking to anybody about her love for him. Anyway, he was dead and gone. The man she had left her first husband for; the man she had endangered the safe lives of her first two children for; the stepfather they resented, admired, loved, and sometimes hated; the father their shared son loved, admired, resented, and sometimes hated; the man she had lived with, worked with, laughed with, quarreled with, shared every penny with, his or hers; the man she shared bed and board with, day and night, mind and body. Could you call missing all that being horny?

She was suffused with the memory of a night in Florida, in a sleazy place in Clearwater much like this one. She couldn't remember why they were so lucky as to be there alone. No kids—not the two older ones or even their younger one. Probably all left in the care of Grandmother, Abuela, in the larger sleazy place up the beach they had rented for the whole family and a cousin. The Cuban side of Paul's family was jammed with cousins.

One night, one lovely undisturbed night with the love of her life. They had shrimp for dinner at a restaurant on the bay. Then a leisurely walk to the beach, jabbering away. They were both big talkers. Paul had reserved a room in an odd round structure originally conceived as a tropical paradise resort. Built in the twenties, it had bedrooms overlooking a circular court that boasted a palm-thatched bar and dance floor with live band. A central staircase rose to the bedrooms, whose rounded windows romantically faced the ocean. Now the outer walls let the wind and rain in, the dance floor was warped, the bar and band were no more. The Round of Pleasure had been a dream place for Paul in his adolescence. It was a gas to come to it in their middle age.

How she enjoyed him, his effervescent talk, his brilliant laughter, the angry, funny play of his mind, his long, lean, strong form, his full cushioned lips, his tongue, his electric hands, the silky hair covering his body, the more wonderful silk of his penis. And his feet. His beautiful feet.

Yes. And not to forget the violent temper, the sulky childishness, the ego, the lust for recognition of his work—*my work, my work*—the restlessness, the incessant demand that he be Numero Uno, the deliberately inflicted hurts when he imagined she had humiliated him. She hadn't forgotten. She wasn't romanticizing her life with Paul. She had loved him with her eyes wide open for the man that he was, not some dreamboat she invented after he was dead.

They had had a good time together. A good life. She never wanted it to end. Why couldn't it have gone on forever?

He's dead, she told herself, and felt her body lifeless. *He died at age seventy-eight of prostate cancer. Your mother and father are dead. All your brothers are dead. And Naomi is on her way, and Eva, and Flora is eighty-five and you're eighty. Nobody lives forever. Don't be a child. Get on with what you have to do.*

What do I have to do? Hopelessly awake, she thought again of Naomi's whispered on-and-off request. She clicked off tomorrow's chores: calls to her children to tell them she was fine, calls to doctors, a phone conference with Eva's children, a visit to Naomi's bank, more quarrels with Flora.

Eva's bloated, hairy face appeared. What were they doing to her? What were they medicating her with? Elegant, grown-up Eva. Already married when Jenny was six years old, settled into a life complete with husband, children, and even a girl from Ireland to help with the housework. Her comfortable apartment was a refuge for adolescent sulks as Jenny grew up in turn. Eva helped her find her way in the world.

She even gave Jenny money for extravagances, gave her a dollar fifty to see the first live play she had ever seen, *Cyrano de Bergerac*, with a terrible ham actor whose name she had forgotten. Long-lived Eva. Had her husband of fifty-six years been the love of her life? Impossible to tell. Eva never talked intimacies. She listened. What a comfort to talk to Eva, who knew how to listen. Carrying on her steady, responsible life, always there for Jenny when Jenny needed her. She had two children as solid in their lives as Eva had been, and from the two, a bumper crop of eight grandchildren, fourteen great-grandchildren, all doing what they were expected to do. Eva talked of them, but not too much. Eva, correct in all her ways.

And what of Flora? Flora's love life? Four marriages—five, technically. She had been married twice to one husband. Three divorces, one annulment. Two husbands now dead. Two floating around, one a good old friend, but infirm, the other lost somewhere. Four children, three grandchildren. She had had other men in her bed, too many to keep track of. Flora used the word "love" a lot. "He fell in love with me." "I'm in love with him." "We're in love." Along with the down-to-earth talk. "He

can't get it up. He's the original limp-penis guy."
"He wouldn't know a clitoris from a clementine, he
thinks nipples are strictly for babies, he's a two-
minute-flat guy." Often about the same man. "He's
passionately in love with me, but the poor thing
can't get it up, no matter what I do to help." "He
used to be good a couple of years ago, real good, but
medication or something did him in, he can't do a
thing anymore. It would be sad if it weren't funny,
because he's desperately in love with me."

Any of those the love of Flora's life? And what
if there were no such thing as the love of one's life?
If Jenny's own sexual existence had been nothing
but romantic illusion? How about those geese who
mated for life? Was she the only monogamous
human being on earth? (Leaving aside her first marriage, when she was too young to know which end
was up.) Because she couldn't swear for Paul, naturally. She knew Paul had loved her. But apparently
exclusive love could be a straitjacket. There were no
open signs of others in her husband's life. She had
never asked. She was afraid of the answer?

And then there was Naomi's love life. Women,
men, old men when she was young, young men when
she was old, at least one black and one Asian (but who

was counting colors?), a gay man offering companionship and marriage but no sex, a husband of twenty years, a pickup on the boardwalk when she was in her eighties, of a suave Italian con man looking for marriage, the whole stormy relationship complete with sex, lies, professions of love, theft of a diamond ring, betrayal, and an operatic breakup. Two long-ago abortions, illegal. Two marriages, one annulment. No children. The love of Naomi's life? Another question Jenny didn't ask. Naomi would probably name Sam, her handsome musician husband.

Sleep, sleep, if only she could fall asleep. She lit the dim lamp over the bed and propped up the slippery pillows, hoping that the two current magazines she had brought with her would tire her eyes enough to put her out. Instead everything she read stirred her up. The newsweekly bits were horrifying—unthinkable killings, scandals, betrayals personal and public, national and international. She switched to the slicker magazine. She couldn't understand most of the cartoons—their references were a mystery. *I've lived too long*, she thought, and dropped the periodicals over the side of the bed.

* * *

When Jenny came back to the funky motel after a good enough breakfast at a health-food bar, there was a message from Flora to call her at once. She didn't. She would do the research into Naomi's bank accounts first.

She took a bus that was filled with passengers, though it was after nine o'clock. Her white hair immediately earned her a seat given up by a young woman tourist. The breezy, sunny morning had lured the foreign tourists out in their vigorously sporty outfits, newly tanned legs and arms bared, noses burned red, light-colored eyes opened wide to the wonders. Across the aisle was a very old Jewish woman in an all-black outfit, her scrawny legs exposed in black tights, her scrawny ass barely covered by a black skirt, her face masked by makeup, her hair drawn up into a wide-brimmed felt hat, her poor feet stuffed into papery boots with stiletto heels. A Flora type, but worse. There were a couple of the usual seedy men who seemed to be perpetually coming from or going to the track, and there was the usual mix of languages, colors of skin. The bus driver was black but didn't speak. Unidentifiable. Two middle-aged women deep in a lively conversation in Spanish sat near a group of quiet youngsters, male and female look-alikes, toting backpacks. A young man in a yarmulke leafed through *Esquire*.

Their route took them along a wide boulevard skirting a waterway lined with yachts, some for sale, some private, some large excursion yachts available for day trips. On the opposite side of the boulevard the condominiums and hotels soared in their fantasy shapes and embellishments: pyramids of Egypt, camels, swans, immense carved giraffes, a building whose huge pillars supporting the entranceway were the draped bodies of slaves. Fun and pleasure. Miami life was all about eating, drinking, loafing, swimming, boating, driving, tanning, conning, fucking, shopping, dancing, praying.

And dying.

The bus made a sharp right across a bridge into an area of chic little shops, restaurants, doctors' offices, banks, a church, an imposing new synagogue. Naomi's bank was on a corner of this broad tree-lined avenue. Jenny had been here on an earlier visit, before the first breast cancer operation, when Naomi had wanted Jenny on all her accounts "just in case." That was a year and a half ago. The decor was the same—plush, comfortable armchairs and sofas, little tables, coffee served, good lavatories—but the very pleasant Cuban woman Jenny had dealt with then was gone.

The woman now handling Naomi's accounts was a Russian Jewish émigré who spoke excellent English. Her open face had a Middle American look, with its fair-skinned, blue-eyed evenness and its beauty parlor hairdo. Her slightly overweight body was neatly held together in a light-green polyester suit, and she wore a gold chain at her neck and gold hoops on her earlobes. Jenny chatted with her about her move from Minsk to Miami Beach. She had studied English all through school back in the Soviet Union. It was a popular language there, lots of students took English. She had come to the United States because she loved *freedom*—the word as she pronounced it appeared in italics. She also loved Miami Beach. She had come seven years ago. She didn't miss Russia, no, and anyway it was very bad there now, she had family and friends, they were suffering, they didn't know from one day to the next what would happen. Economically. Nobody cared about politics anymore. But economics, that was a different story.

She praised Naomi. "Mrs. Rybinski is a lady. A lot of these women at her age, they're hard to deal with, but Mrs. Rybinski is a lady. We never have any trouble. It's a pleasure to deal with your sister. She likes to know what her balance is maybe a little too much, every few days, but she's a lady when she asks." She paused, proudly presenting Jenny with her business card, on which her name appeared as Tatyana Weiss. She invited Jenny to call her Anna. "More American," she said. "Easier to pronounce." Everything between them was pleasantries until her face closed down against whatever she was reading on the computer screen.

"You're Flora Strauss's sister?"

"Yes," Jenny said.

"How many sisters are you?" Tatyana Weiss seemed to be continuing their casual conversation, but her expression was suddenly formal.

"Four, actually, counting myself."

"And your name is . . .?"

"Jane Witter," Jenny said. "I'm on my sister's accounts. I'm the name on my sister's accounts."

But the pleasant face had entirely closed itself off. "I can't give you any information about Mrs. Rybinski's accounts," it said, and turned aside as if the transaction had been completed.

"I don't understand," Jenny said.

"That's the only information I can give you."

"That's preposterous."

"Bank policy," the woman said. "Have a good day."

"Can you tell me if I am listed on my sister's accounts?"

"No information," the woman repeated. "Bank policy."

"I filed a power of attorney with you. For my ninety-year-old sister. Are you telling me that it's no longer operative?"

"Yes, madam. It is no longer operative."

"And I'm no longer on her accounts?"

"I can give you no further information."

"Can she do that? Change everything? Without notifying me? And how about the bank—shouldn't you have notified me? Or something? Doesn't the bank have any responsibility? To me? To the fact that the woman is ninety years old?"

"Would you like to see the manager? He will be available after two o'clock. That's all I can do for you, madam."

"What's the matter?" Jenny said. "We were a couple of human beings a few moments ago. What happened? I'm just trying to determine the state of my ninety-year-old sister's accounts."

"Have a good day, madam." Tatyana Weiss picked up her phone and turned her back on Jenny altogether, gathering up the remains of their formerly friendly paper cups of coffee.

There was nothing to do but face Naomi. Jenny had spent weeks with Naomi during the first breast operation, seeing doctors, lawyers, bank reps, checking on CDs, Dreyfus, money market investments, getting the power of attorney and the medical papers virtually putting her in charge of Naomi's life and death. "Just in case," Naomi had said. But Naomi had made a remarkable recovery. Until the cancer flared up again eight months later.

What was going on? Was she going to have to go through that whole song and dance again? Had Naomi said "just in case" to someone else? When *just in case* was clearly so much nearer now, had Naomi displaced her sister Jenny with a nearer and dearer *just in case*? Was it Flora? It had to be Flora. But it couldn't be Flora, because for all her faults Flora wouldn't prey on Naomi's fears to muscle in on her money. It must be someone outside the family, trying to take advantage of Naomi. Retirement homes were always after their residents' assets, Jenny knew.

She decided to walk to Naomi's residence, a distance of about a mile. Though the sun was hotter, there was still a pleasant breeze. The shops had let down their awnings, and Jenny strolled, telling herself she was enjoying the splashy displays in the shopwindows. The fact was, a familiar bitterness had invaded her system, spoiling everything. Family. What a mess.

She found Naomi in the formerly elegant, dreary lobby, dressed in another silk ensemble, blue with white dots, full skirt, loose jacket, the ornate gold watch she had bought at Nieman Marcus heavy on its braided chain against her poor mutilated chest, her pretty face framed in another brimmed cotton hat pulled low over her hazel eyes.

"Jenny," she called out. "Here, I'm here, I'm here," and fussed with the lock of her wheelchair. "Where's Flora? She called me at seven-thirty this morning and told me you'd moved out. You have to understand, Jenny, I can't, I'm too old, who's right, who's wrong, I can't anymore. Are you mad at me?"

Jenny laughed and kissed her.

Naomi's eyes filled with tears. "You're not mad at me?"

"I'm the little sister," Jenny said. "I just do as I'm told."

"You're mad at me." Naomi let the tears overflow a little. "Flora said she'd come right after her exercise class."

"When would that be?" Jenny asked.

"About an hour. How is Eva? How did you find her?"

"You know," Jenny said. "That medication—"

"I know. Like a balloon. And the hair all over her face. My poor sister."

"Let's go out on the terrace."

Jenny wheeled Naomi through a series of hallways into the sea air, having first fetched a woolen shawl and a fine blanket to protect Naomi from the breeze. They sat under the shade of the palm trees because the sun also bothered Naomi. The boardwalk and the beach below were gay with vacationers. Little boats bobbed, the great boats claimed the horizon, the horizon yielded to the clear blue sky, the sky arched to fill the whole happy scene.

Naomi had turned sullen. "I called my bank. I needed to know my checking account balance.

They told me you were there, that my sister had been there asking questions."

"I wanted to make sure everything was in order," Jenny said.

"You weren't here. What was I supposed to do? I didn't even know if you were coming. You're always so busy, running around, lecturing, that stuff that's so important to you. I couldn't be sure you'd come. What was I supposed to do, with this operation next week? I just wish I could die before next week, I wish I could just go off in my sleep, smiling. I always meant to go out smiling."

She wasn't smiling now. She was if anything black with anger.

"I don't care what you think of me, Jenny. I know you don't think much of me, but that's okay. That's perfectly okay. It's no more than I expect."

"I love you," Jenny said. "I think the world of you."

There was a fuss going on at the other end of the terrace near the unused bar. Something about a chair. "You know that's my chair, that's the chair I always use," a frail old woman was shouting in a surprisingly strong voice. "So why do you take it? Why do you deliberately take my chair when you know

I'm coming any minute to use it." Another voice kept repeating in tones of wonder, "Did you ever see such a nerve? Did you ever experience such a nerve in your life? Such a nerve?"

"Stop listening to those idiots," Naomi yelled at Jenny. "We're trying to have a talk here." She cried a few more tears, dabbing at her eyes. The blackness was fading. She looked into Jenny's face with an expression more like fear. "Am I going to lose you now? Will you go back right away now?"

"Why would I do that?"

"Because of the money. Because I changed all the accounts."

Jenny felt a stab of apprehension but forced herself to speak calmly. "Naomi, your money is your money to do what you think best with. I just think you might have told me. I made a fool of myself at your bank this morning." And fresh bitterness flowed through her. It had been worse than that. She had felt like a moneygrubber. As if she were after Naomi's money.

Am I after Naomi's money? The thought stopped Jenny cold. And then, *Better me than the residence.*

"Listen, Jenny," Naomi said in a rush. "Here, I made out a check to you this morning for twenty thousand dollars. I arranged it all over the phone. I moved some money from my investment account to my checking account. It's absolutely sound. A sound check. I want you to have it. I don't need it, I don't need any more money. Take it, take it. If you can't use it, give it to your children. I always loved them, you know that. Take it, please, you can't refuse me, you have to take it." And was again in tears.

"Naomi, I was just trying to make sure your accounts were safe. I don't want any money. I just wanted to know what's available so that you can have everything you need, so there's money enough for whatever you need."

"I don't need anything. I wish I was dead."

"You don't mean that," Jenny said.

"Oh God, you're angry with me. I know you're angry with me. Are you going to leave me? I can't do this alone, Jenny, I can't. I don't know why I listened to her in the first place. Sometimes I don't even know what she's talking about. I'm so tired, I just give in. You know how she is with her advice advice advice. I want you to have it, if not you, then your children. She doesn't have to know."

"Who? Whose advice? Who doesn't have to know?"

"Flora, Flora, of course—who else? Please take the check, take it, take, I want you to have it."

Flora. Flora after all. Jenny reached out and took the check. She folded it in half and put it in the zipper compartment of her small Coach bag.

"Thank you," she said.

"Use it in good health," Naomi mumbled.

"Thank you," Jenny said again, and amazed herself by busily figuring what proportion of Naomi's money she had just received and how much was still controlled by Flora. Forty thousand? At the most. Naomi didn't have much.

She amazed herself by her resolution, too. If there was going to be a tug of war for Naomi's money, she wasn't going to let Flora win. Flora had plenty of money. Flora didn't need any more money. Jenny had a lot less money than Flora. Oh, she had enough, but enough for what? What if she lived as long as Eva? Or as long as Naomi? Ten years, fifteen years more? Wouldn't she need more money?

She didn't give a damn about comparative need. She was determined to win. She didn't care how awful she was being. She would win this family fight no matter what. She wasn't going to let Flora win this one.

3

HEROIC MEASURES

A family party took place for Eva's ninety-fifth birthday, which had actually gone by two weeks earlier without celebration. Jenny, in the midst of the business of settling Naomi's accounts so that they were firmly under her thumb, found herself oddly looking forward to it.

Eva's daughter was in charge, a generally loved and admired relative in the family. A large, handsome woman in her early seventies, she was a gifted diplomat, so that even the four sisters felt equally stroked and comforted, and with her good managerial skills she directed the details of the dinner unobtrusively. It was held at Eva's retirement residence in a private dining room just beyond the ornate main one. The guest list was small, considering the size of the family. There were eighteen people at a long table, nicely laid with flower baskets and candles, everybody dressed up, celebratory. Even Flora was almost appropriate in a silk shift of sedate banded colors, though glittered up with gold shoes and thigh-high gilt stockings that tended to slip down her legs. She wore a long string of fake oversize pearls that bounced about when she moved, and she moved constantly. The black blackness of her hair was startling.

There was a minimum of wheelchairs at the table—Eva's, Naomi's, and one for a friend of Eva's from the residence—and only two walkers, also for the use of Eva's friends, and a couple of canes. But the seating of Eva became a hassle. She refused the head of the table, where she had first been wheeled.

"I won't be able to hear what anybody is saying except the persons on my left and right. I want to hear what everybody is saying. It's my party, and I want to hear what's going on."

Finally fixed in the middle of the long table, she became engrossed in the question of seating others, and in the quality of the menu.

"This must be costing a fortune," she said in a loud whisper to her daughter. "It better not show up on my bill, that's all I have to say." And said it a number of times.

She wore a handsome black-and-white pantsuit, but it was slung on her wasted body as if on a wire hanger, and with her moon face even her careful hairdo and makeup could not erase the deformation. She repeatedly questioned her daughter in a whisper everyone heard.

"Who invited *him?*"

Nieces and nephews she seldom saw were a special target.

"Who invited *her?* I guess she came for the food. She's not fooling me, not one bit. I know why she came. They come if it's convenient," she ventured between wine toasts to her continuing years. "They live nearby, so they come. For the food. Look how they're eating. Otherwise you wouldn't see them."

Relatives who lived in Florida had been urged to appear to make the occasion sufficiently gala. Only Eva's children and a couple of her grandchildren had come from distant points, her son and daughter for reasons other than the party, the son from Philadelphia, the daughter from Colorado, to settle questions of health care, of the sale of Eva's holdings, of what to do next about doctors, medication, permanent care until death. Eva's grandson had come from Albuquerque. He was a middle-aged man, almost bald, tall and muscular, handsome, loving and attentive to Grandma's slightest wish, an obvious favorite. The granddaughter was a Botticelli in a flowered dress that flowed from her lovely bosom down to her feet, big in long black flats. Her fair hair, loose around her classically beautiful face, was pushed behind her ears to cascade down her graceful back. She looked in her twenties, though Jenny knew she was in her late thirties, the mother of three of Eva's great-grandchildren, and a professor of art history at the University of Pennsylvania.

"I wear my hair up in a bun in class, Aunt Jenny," she said when Jenny teased about students trying to date her.

"*Great*-aunt Jenny," her brother corrected, and lifted his glass in a salute. He loved the idea of family, of greats and great-greats. Jenny had visited his house, complete with old family pictures carefully framed and hung. "And of course the kids try to date her," he added.

The service was slow, but there was already much on the table. They drank wine, mineral water, ginger ale; ate bread, challa, and butter; amused themselves with pickles, coleslaw, sauerkraut, apple-sauce, black and green olives, sticks of celery and carrots, and a tasty corn mixture.

"We'll be full before they serve dinner," Flora

said, and proposed another toast to Eva, this one to the artist in Eva, in every woman, in every man, in all life, the artistry with which mankind and womankind lived their lives "as Eva has done, as Eva is doing right now, living out her days as a work of art. May she live till one hundred years."

"What did she say?" Eva said. "What was Flora mumbling about? If she isn't the center of attention she's not happy. So let her be happy, whatever she said. What did she say?"

But the fruit cup arrived and claimed Eva's full concentration. Chicken soup with matzo balls followed quickly, and then there was another long pause. Naomi filled this one. She had written a poem in praise of Eva, her theme the great distances people had traveled to be present. Some of it rhymed, some didn't.

> Everybody is dressed nicely,
> All the food is good and spicy.
> Nephew Samuel came all the way from Atlanta,
> Great-niece Carol called on the phone,
> For it was too far from Montana.
> Maine was Jenny's starting place,
> A year ago it could have been Spain.

A long poem, made longer by Naomi's halting reading and the audience's interruptions of appreciation. Some of it was unintelligible to Jenny, but the ending came through clearly.

> *We all love Eva,*
> *Long may she wave*
> *O'er the Miami land of the free*
> *And the Miami home of the brave.*

Under cover of the applause and laughter someone said, "Isn't that a football team?" And Jenny heard Eva complaining, "I couldn't hear a word, not a word. What did she say? She looks beautiful, I'll say that for her."

Naomi did indeed look beautiful, in dress, hat, manner, serene face and carriage. She had been silent before reading the poem and was silent afterwards, turning from speaker to speaker with her large, intelligent eyes fixed on their faces, smiling, smiling, smiling—at Eva, at the relatives, at the waiters, at her own reflection in a compact mirror, at Jenny across the table, and again at her own reflection.

Following the chicken, potatoes, mixed vegetables, salad, and compote came the birthday cake, complete with the blowing out of the candles after the "Happy Birthday" song, in which the staff and waiters joined. Then coffee and tea (decaffeinated) and a round of champagne.

Jenny felt Eva's exhaustion even as Eva forced herself to rise to the occasion. For a few minutes, with a great effort of will and memory, Eva became the woman she had always been in social situations—alert, elegant, and gracious. In a clear, strong voice, she thanked everybody for coming, for their gifts of flowers and their good wishes, and in turn wished them "all the good things of life" and a very, very good night, before inexplicably reverting to irritability when her daughter announced that the party was shifting to "the ballroom."

"I'm too tired. And what about the flowers? Take, take, everyone, we don't want them to go to waste, and I can't use all these flowers. Come on, come on, come on, I'm tired, let's get this over with."

Shepherded by Eva's daughter, everyone moved in a clumsy body, by wheelchairs, walkers, canes, and legs, to a large room off the central lobby where live music was being supplied by a group of half-live musicians. There was a good-sized waxed floor, with some surprisingly athletic old couples dancing. It was the Villa Rosa's regular Saturday night dance, decorated with miniature silver top hats, confetti, balloons, and ivory cigarette holders dangling from the ceiling.

"They try to make it feel like the twenties when we were all young. Some try." Eva, dripping scorn.

There were prizes and refreshments at a long table, a special area for wheelchairs and walkers, and a small platform for the decrepit five-man band. The saxophonist was deathly white. Each intake of breath might be his last, and the drummer, his heavy body swaying and yearning toward the floor, made Jenny nervous.

"They make fools of themselves here every Saturday night," Eva said, "but what the hell, I come and watch them anyway."

Eva's Botticelli granddaughter electrified the room and was seized on by a thin, stooped old man who had been dancing around the floor alone. She begged off, he persisted passionately and won. He didn't try to embrace her in a traditional lead, but danced in the current style, without touching, facing her. In a black pinstripe suit too big for his wasted body, his tie loosened, his white hair fluttering, his limbs as if screwed in at the wrong angle, his feet dragging, his back bent almost double, no longer able to convey rhythm with his wreck of a body, he used whatever he had left, kept time with a raised index finger, greeted the draggy music with an eloquent dip of his drooping head, marked the beat with a defining stamp of one aching foot, his face ecstatic, his shoulders rolling, a dancer to the end, which might seize him at any instant. Meanwhile, he treasured his turn with his enchanting springtime youth in her long flowered dress and flowing hair, stumbling about in her large flat-heeled shoes, embarrassed as hell.

Jealous, Flora cut in during the pause between dance numbers, dismissing Eva's granddaughter and steering the momentarily bewildered old man into a fast step.

"You're leading me," he hollered, trying to escape Flora's grip. She was holding him by both arms, moving him around expertly. Flora was still a terrific dancer. "Stop it, stop it. I'm the leader. The man is the leader. Let go of me. I want my partner, my real partner."

He broke free, located his Botticelli, and without touching her lured her back to the floor. Once again youth and age danced. Flora, outraged by a public rejection, began circling the couple in a frenzy of rapid steps and high kicks, slapping her hand to the inside of her elbow and raising her arm in alternation with fluttering hand-to-nose signals accompanied by crooning cries of "Fuck you, old man" in tune with the music. Her silk dress had fallen over one shoulder, exposing her bra strap, her hair was a soot-black mess, her slip showed its lacy edge, and her gilt thigh-highs were sliding into her gilded shoes.

"She's wonderful!" Jenny heard a woman exclaim. "She's as good as Twyla Tharp."

Even those in the residence who wanted to hate it loved it: the family of correct, sedate Eva Resnick making a show of themselves. *Scandale.* Entrancing. Better than a show, better than a musical. "If you paid sixty-five dollars a ticket like on Broadway, it couldn't be better," one woman said. Jenny heard others take up the refrain like a mantra and repeat it again and again.

"I'm very tired," Naomi said. "This is exhausting."

It was Eva who broke the spell. "Enough is enough. *Fini la comédie.* Naomi's tired. So am I. Time for bed. Let's say these festivities are at an end.

Definitively." And gestured for someone to move her wheelchair in the right direction. Out of that ballroom. Out.

"I don't want her money," Flora said. "But why should a nursing home get it? You secure it, I don't care, I just don't want the nursing home to get it. You know what they charge? Five, six, seven thousand a month, depending on the billing, depending on what they can stick you with, aspirin, X-rays, the nurses' gloves, for God's sake. Seventeen dollars a box and they bill you for gloves every few days. I know the ropes. I have plenty of friends in nursing homes."

"We can't secure the money if you mean hide it," Jenny said. "You mean Medicaid, putting her on Medicaid? They do a three-year back search. Through all holdings, all accounts, all financial transactions. It's too late to hide her money."

"I know all about the three-year back search. You get around it. Everybody does. You think people are paying those terrible amounts of money? Nobody's paying. They all go on Medicaid."

"I don't see how," Jenny said. "Naomi told me

that she doesn't even want to go to a convalescent home after the operation next week. I had a long talk with her. She says she'll only stay in the hospital overnight, and then back to the residence. I think she'd die in five minutes in a Medicaid space in an old age home."

"A nursing home," Flora corrected. "It's not a question of what Naomi wants, it's a question of the right thing to do. How does she expect to go back to the residence? She can't go down to meals. They've been carrying her meals up to her room. Five dollars a clip, she insists on giving them five dollars a clip. She can't manage by herself now, how is she going to manage after the operation? She's not going to get better, you know. She's dying, Jenny. The doctor said six months, if that. And she's making a mess of it. She spent seventy-five hundred on her funeral expenses. Okay, so everything's arranged, casket, shipment to New York, the whole bit, but she didn't have to spend more than four thousand. I gave her the best information, no, she had to go to the place she wanted, she knew better, she had to go to the place she wanted just so she could be overcharged."

"Oh," Jenny said, at a loss. And went back to the beginning. "Putting your name on her accounts doesn't make them yours, Flora. You understand? They'll still come after Naomi to pay her bills, or they'll come after you if your name is on the accounts. If the money's there, you have to pay."

"They can't make a sister responsible." Flora, triumphant. "I checked that. It's the law."

"But it's *her* money. They're *her* accounts, Naomi's accounts. They can't make you use your money, but they can make us use hers."

"You don't know a thing about money, Jenny. You never did and you never will. All I was trying to do was save Naomi some money, which God knows is hard enough. You know what she did last week? Ordered an eighty-dollar nightgown from Lord and Taylor. Ever hear of such a thing? And promptly had a hemorrhage from that wound on her leg from the last operation that never healed. That nightgown's ruined. Eighty-five dollars thrown in the garbage."

"You said eighty," Jenny interrupted before she could stop herself.

"Eighty, eighty-five. I'm just trying to save that foolish woman some money."

"What for, if she's dying?"

"Are you crazy? Why should her money go down the drain? Why should it go to the nursing home if she could stay there free? Everybody else does it that way. Give away the money to children, sisters, whatever, and go in for free."

"But it's too late. It would be a hassle now. They'd search her accounts. They'd go after the money she has."

"You don't know a thing about money, Jenny, but if you don't want to listen to someone who does, that's fine. I don't care. I don't care what you do. You and Naomi between you do whatever you like. You want to do everything wrong, go ahead, you don't have to listen to me. Make all the mistakes you want to, throw her money in the garbage if that's what you want."

"All I want is to do things the way Naomi wants them done. And to have the money to do them with. Which Naomi has if we just leave her money alone."

"Whatever, whatever, whatever," Flora said. "You want to throw good money after bad, go right ahead, be my guest. Now do you mind, I'm exhausted, I have to take a nap."

It was two in the afternoon. Flora had been undressing during the sisters' conversation. She had always slept naked, Jenny remembered. Flesh-pink naked now, she walked from bureau to closet, dressing again, in a long nightshirt, socks, a scarf at her throat, and a little crocheted hat for her head. "I get very cold sleeping lately." She pulled down the dark purple blinds against the sun blazing off the sea and opened one of the windows slightly, letting in a warm whistling wind.

"Isn't that breeze delicious?" she said.

Actually, it was smelly, but Jenny couldn't tell of what. A faintly garbagy odor, mixed with barbecuing meat and sea mist.

Flora said, pulling back the bedcover, "Could you turn off the air conditioning on your way out? I put it on just for you. I know you like it cold. And slam the door, it locks automatically. Thanks." She closed her eyes and turned her back, snuggling under the fluffy lilac blanket.

At the apartment door Jenny stopped when Flora called out, "Listen, I forgot. I have a date tonight. Fascinating man. Used to own a very smart jewelry store on Lincoln Road, when Lincoln Road was Lincoln Road. Picked me up there, actually, a couple of days ago. He's desperately in love with me. I only hope he can get it up. Anyway, I'm busy tonight, and I figured you'd have supper with Naomi. Okay?"

"Okay," Jenny said. "Have fun. And be careful."

"I won't, I won't, I won't be careful," Flora yelled as Jenny closed the door. "I'll be damned if I'll be careful. Be careful, be careful, be careful. The hell with that. That's all I ever hear from you. Be careful, be good, be careful. The hell with it."

In the hushed, carpeted corridor, a young Latina with a sleeping child in a collapsible stroller was letting herself into the apartment opposite Flora's. She smiled, shrugged, gestured in a marvelously eloquent statement of understanding, and disappeared behind her own door. But what the whole pantomime meant was hard for Jenny to decipher. Flora was a nut? She, Jenny, was the nut, to be placated with smiles, shrugs, and hand motions? The performance had nothing to do with content but was an expression of Latino delicacy, a bonding, an acceptance of yelling as a natural part of family life? Whatever it all meant, it was soothing.

Outside, walking rapidly in the direction of her drab room, she tried to think through the whole mess. First, she had been wrong about Flora's motive in changing the accounts. There wasn't any motive, just Flora being officious and know-it-all, trying to save a buck. Handling Naomi's money wisely, saving Naomi's money. To what end?

What did Naomi want? Peace, quiet. She didn't want to go anywhere. She didn't want to go to the hospital for another operation, she didn't want to move to a convalescent center where she would never get any better, only worse, and end up in a pissy nursing-home dying ward in a pissy Medicaid bed. She wanted to be left alone. She wanted to stay in her 1920s run-down residence and pretend she was a guest in an elegant hotel, dressing in her charming outfits, graciously tipping the help, picking up her mail at the desk, calling for a taxi, sitting in the lobby, dining at her reserved table, taking the air on the terrace, gently aloof and superior to all the other guests, pulling her cotton print hat down to shade her hazel eyes, drawing her flowered shawl around her shoulders, keeping intact her idea of herself. Naomi Rybinski, woman of the world.

She wanted to die smiling.

Naomi had given Flora twenty thousand dollars. Jenny had learned that much from Naomi's bankbook and her frightened explanations. She had responded to a kind of blackmail on Flora's part: *Do as I say or I won't have anything more to do with you.* She paid the money to keep Flora near her. She put Flora on her accounts to keep Flora at her side. She gave Flora twenty thousand dollars as insurance against being left to die alone. Jenny hadn't been on the scene, so Naomi had dumped her. She had replaced Jenny's name with Flora's. If that was what Flora wanted, then yes yes yes, anything, anything not to be left to die alone.

Well then, what about the twenty thousand Naomi had given Jenny? Jenny was back, Jenny had returned, as promised. Whose promises were safer? Maybe keeping her money floating in the reach of both sisters was the safest thing to do, like corporations contributing to both the Democratic and Republican parties. Insurance.

How much money was left?

Could Jenny convince Flora that both of them should put their twenty-thousand-dollar gifts back in Naomi's account?

That was the thing to do, so that the money would be available as needed. Preferably with Jenny's name on the accounts. Of course with her name on the accounts. Wasn't it she who had always been there for Naomi? She would blackmail Naomi as cruelly as Flora had: *Do as I say or else—*

Between us we'll murder her, she thought. *Flora with her cockamamie ideas about the proper use of money. And you? What's your interest? Not the money, not the money, not the money*, she hoped. Yes, the money, who was she kidding, but money for Naomi first, money for Naomi's comfort and care, for her use in any damn way she chose. Half a dozen Lord and Taylor nightgowns if that was what Naomi wanted. And if something was left over, some of the money left after Naomi was gone, wouldn't Jenny deserve it? Well, wouldn't she? If she did everything right through to the end?

She was tired. She had walked eight or ten blocks into an area of small stores, beauty parlors, laundries and dry cleaners, money changers, restaurants, American, Cuban, Italian, kosher, Indian, Chinese, seafood, fast food, health food, alongside a heavily trafficked road. A roofed bus stop offered refuge from the sun and a no-back bench missing one of its slats. She sat, breathed deeply, enjoyed the wind and the shade. There was the usual mix of people waiting for the bus, all colors, classes, sexes, styles. They all took the first bus that came along.

Jenny sat on alone. In the sickly shrubbery bordering the bus stop, trash bloomed: pissed-on newspapers, plastic bags, food packaging, remains of pizzas, chicken, hotdogs, unidentifiable messes, soda cans, beer bottles, wine and liquor bottles. Toward the curb, around a standing refuse bin, garbage was rampant. She sat on, hypnotized, dazed. New bus riders collected: a small, round Latina with a child in her arms and two more trailing, all in clean white University of Nebraska T-shirts, eating candy, tossing the wrappers under the bench; another tense, skinny middle-aged man on his way to the track, or home from it without a cent, alongside a totally silent woman with a fixed smile suggesting that she might be with him, though it was hard to tell; a highly coiffed woman in a maize pantsuit, carrying a large Victoria's Secret shopping bag and dropping crumpled tissues behind the bench; a fat young woman eating a pizza, in torn cutoffs and what looked like a plain white five-and-dime brassiere; a neat blond nurse unwrapping a stick of gum; an old black man in washed and pressed cotton pants and short-sleeved shirt, singing to himself in Spanish, tossing his newspaper on the bench.

Cut, Jenny thought. *Enough. I'm ready for a new*

video. I'm tired of this scene and this action. I'm not watching the neat nurse surreptitiously drop the gum wrapper in the shrubbery. And the pizza eater? Will she use the trash can? I don't want to see her dump her crusts under the bench. I want the end to this endless video.

And then found herself thinking, with excitement, *If I protected my hands with those Wash'n Dri's I carry around in my bag, I could clean up this garbage.*

It presented itself as a reasonable, manageable job. She could actually do it, clean up this unnecessary street mess. It would be fun. As if in a dream of work, she set to it. Protecting her hands was not so easy. Even with a couple of rubber bands she found stashed away in her handbag, which she twisted around the little wet napkins tucked in at her wrists, it was hard to keep her makeshift gloves in place. Maybe she could walk into a nursing home and steal a pair of rubber gloves? Never mind. The important thing was not to touch the filth. She changed tactics, using the Wash'n Dri's as though she were mopping up gravy with two pieces of bread, shoveling the stuff up from the sidewalk into the almost empty trash can. It was amazing how quickly the state of the sidewalk was improving. Just one person making all this difference. All by herself she was cleaning up. Suddenly stiff from bending, she straightened to rest her back, and as she was admiring her own handiwork, she was stilled by a consciousness of peculiar silence. A crowd had gathered. Not only the people waiting for the bus, but others, out for a walk, doing errands, shopping. Quite a number had stopped in their tracks to watch.

"Crazy. Poor thing's crazy," a woman said.

"*Meshuga ahf toit*," said another.

You could help, she yelled, unable to comprehend what these strangers were doing in her dream. And then, *Yes, Yes. I am, I am, I'm meshuga ahf toit*.

Exactly. Crazed to death.

She ran from the bus stop. Back in her room, she showered vigorously, washing, washing, washing away craziness and filth. She was planning to visit Eva in her residence, and later Naomi in hers. What if she carried exotic germs to infect them? Well, what if she did? Wouldn't it be a mitzva? Wasn't it everybody's unspoken hope that her sisters would die quickly and quietly, and as inexpensively as possible?

She took two aspirin, then dressed in a carefully chosen cream silk outfit, adding dark kid shoes, a multicolored scarf, and the Coach bag. Obliterate that madwoman cleaning up the street. The mirror returned an image of a well-dressed, self-contained, modestly made-up elderly woman with a good hair-cut.

Her daughter called from Vermont, loving and anxious. Jenny had become sufficiently herself to chat reassuringly, though her daughter was not convinced.

"You don't sound right, Mom. Are you okay?"

"I'm fine, darling, I'm fine. It's hard. Four sisters make for a slippery slope, but I'm fine. How are you and Dan and the children?"

"Everybody's great. Kids are great. Dan's busy busy busy, and so am I. I'm worried about you, Mom. Don't overdo, remember you can't save the world. You couldn't do it when you were young, hard as you tried. No chance now when everything is worse. Promise me you'll go home if it becomes unbearable."

"I can't leave your aunt Naomi. I can't leave her alone."

"I know. I wish I could help, but I'm so busy on that new project I told you about. Today is a day from hell. I love it, though, I couldn't possibly pull out right now. And your sons aren't even around.

They're both in Australia, but not together. Isn't that wild?"

"Why is it wild?" There were times when Jenny hardly understood the tack her children's conversation took. "Is something going on I don't know about?"

"No, no, it's just an expression. I meant the coincidence, you know, that they should both be in Australia of all places at the same time in connection with their work." And without a pause, "Shit, there's another call, and I'm late for a meeting. I better go now. I'll call again tomorrow and check on things. Are my cousins down there helping? Eva's kids? I'm sure Aunt Flora's a handful all by herself. Any of her kids around, or aren't they speaking this week? Were all those male cousins of mine clever enough to stay away? Mom, please take care of yourself, don't let them—hell, I know you're the youngest, and I know you're in great shape, but don't forget you're eighty. I'm sorry, but I better take that other call. Bye, Mom, speak to you soon. Feel good."

Jenny hung up. She could see her daughter as clearly as if the phone contained a screen: dear animated face, supple body in black pants, little white shirt or sweater, black jacket, black tights boots gloves, long slim coat, big bag, big hair, big earrings, big gold chain, big blue eyes, quick bright speech, on the run on the run on the run, to work, to work, back home to children and husband, to the kitchen, to the bedroom, to the office, on the phone on the phone on the phone, for business, for friends, for her brothers and for her mother, running running running her heart out, walking walking walking in her fashionable high-heeled black boots, coat flying behind, pushing pushing pushing, on the march to find herself, to be herself, in all the manifestations she was called on to be. A soldier in a great army in a great long battle.

It was Mama who called up the image of woman as soldier, before she died. Jenny had been putting frantic questions, hurrying to understand before it was too late. How did you do it, Mama, seven pregnancies, breast feeding, no money, no help, cleaning, cooking, working in the store, taking over when Papa napped, sewing, knitting, crocheting fine cotton tablecloths, cooking, cleaning, birthing, rearing, breathing love love love day after hard day, night after hard night?

"What could I do? That's what women did. They went on. Like a soldier in battle, fighting to stay alive for your children, hoping for the best, hoping for better to come, doing what has to be done. You think I didn't want to lie down and sleep forever? Plenty of times I wanted to lie down and sleep forever. I said to myself in those days and nights, you're a soldier in a war. If you drop you're dead. You have to keep going. For yourself and for your husband and for the children you brought into the world, because that's your job here in this life. That's your job. To keep going. And that's what I did, I kept going."

They were talking on the porch of the nice little house Mama's rich successful son Max had bought for her and Papa in Miami Beach. Jenny was a young woman. Mama was dying: any moment her heart would stop. She had closed her eyes as if even to speak of those hard times was exhausting. When she opened them, they were refreshed, amazingly young, laughing.

"There were good times. We had our good times, me and Papa. We paid for them, but we had them. I was a fool, an ignoramus. I had no education, nothing, not like you young women of today. Who knows what I could have done in the world? I accomplished nothing. A whole life of *gornisht mit gornisht*. But I stayed alive. I didn't let the battle kill me."

"You had us," Jenny said. "You should have been covered with medals like those stupid generals. You did a lot in the world."

Mama laughed, which turned into uncontrollable coughing, then choking so severe that an ambulance had to be called and there was no more chance to talk before she died a week later, in the hospital, tied to an oxygen tank that could not save her.

The phone rang, waking Jenny from a dream of Naomi that turned nightmare in that instant, though it had seemed oddly natural as a dream. Naomi lying in a hospital bed. Jenny apparently visiting. Naomi covered up to her shoulders in a white sheet, her face composed, and yes, smiling, her greeny hazel eyes peaceful and glowing, her dark hair combed back off her forehead from its innocent part. But when Jenny tried to smooth the sheet over the body, there was no body. Only Naomi's head—beautiful, simple, composed, smiling—cut off like a classic marble bust.

Her heart skittering in her chest, Jenny picked

up the phone. It was Flora, in a conspiratorial voice.

"Jenny, I can't get him out. I'm scared. He has a gun. Can you come over?"

She heard herself asking stupidly, "What time is it?" And then, "Why don't you call the police?"

"No, no." Louder now, more natural. "I can't do that. You don't understand."

She saw on her bedside clock that it was only ten. "Okay," she said. "I have to dress first, then I'll be right there."

"I'm sorry I woke you." Flora was back to her hushed drama voice. "Please hurry, please. I'll leave the door open."

Jenny dressed and descended into the balmy night and the liveliness of the terrace, swimmers in the pool, diners in the cafe, people sitting around talking and laughing, kids running and yelling. Unreal. She seemed unable to plan how to get to Flora's condominium. Luckily a cab delivered a group of foreign tourists. The driver insisted he was on call farther north, but Jenny pleaded emergency and that her destination was very near. She fingered a five-dollar bill, hinting at a big tip, though when it came to paying she gave him only seventy-five cents. He had driven wildly, mumbling angrily throughout the short drive. The hell with him. She was sick of surly cab drivers.

The Indian security guard at Flora's condominium wanted to ring the apartment, but Jenny persuaded him to let her go up unannounced. He recognized her as Flora's sister. The door was open, as Flora had promised. She pushed into the apartment with her heart banging. It was quiet and very hot. There was light coming from the bedroom, but no sound. In the dimness the softened purples were a stage effect. The sound of the sea was another.

Jenny didn't know what to do. She was a character in some dumb movie, without a script, without a clue. If she charged in, would this Lincoln Road pickup of Flora's shoot her dead? Or shoot Flora dead? Should she lock the door behind her? Call out? Tiptoe into the bedroom? Should she have brought the cops?

Flora appeared in the little hallway from the bedroom, naked, carrying a white terrycloth robe.

"God," she said in her loud normal voice. "You scared me to death. How'd you get past security? Some security. You can't depend on anything or anybody these days. How'd you get in? Did I give you a key to the apartment? I don't remember giving you a key to the apartment. I'll have to have that back if you have one."

Flora was carrying a glass of colorless liquid. Water? Vodka? There was no suggestion of the hushed woman on the phone.

"Are you alone?" Jenny said. "I don't have a key. Don't you remember calling me?"

"Are you crazy? Of course I remember calling you."

"Well, where is he? Is he still here?"

"Of course not," Flora said. "Do you think I'd be so calm?"

Jenny sat down, her legs trembling, her heart shaking wildly.

"What's the matter with you? Are you all right? Do you need some water?"

"Yes," Jenny said. "A glass of cold water. It's very hot in here."

"I know. You like the cold. The air, the water. Ice water. Air conditioning. Shall I turn on the air? I don't like it too cold myself."

"He left? Quietly? What about the gun?"

"Here's your water. Shall I turn on the air? Answer me about the air, because I can do without it. What about the gun? What about it?"

Jenny sipped the water, slowing her heart, cooling her head. She pressed the icy glass against her hot cheek, first one side, then the other, and when she turned her attention again to Flora she found her sister slumped against a wall, sobbing.

"I don't care, I don't care what you think of me. I know very well what you think of me, and I don't give a damn."

Shorter and slighter than Flora, Jenny nevertheless rose to the occasion, getting out of her chair with difficulty and gathering the fleshy terry-wrapped bundle into her arms, rocking and soothing, shushing and smoothing away the sisters' common anguish that none of them really valued the others.

"What happened, darling? He didn't hurt you, did he? That's all that matters. You're safe now, you're okay—unless you're hurt. Are you hurt?"

"My soul is hurt," Flora moaned. "My soul, my woman's soul." And asked for a tissue.

Fetching the tissues was an excuse for Jenny to check out the bedroom and the two bathrooms. They were empty of a man with a gun. Had he ever existed? She heard Flora emoting from the living room.

"What am I going to do? What can I do? I must have love, I must. But men are nothing but trouble. He went crazy when he couldn't get it up. He went out of his mind, stamping around the apartment waving the gun. I think we had too much to drink. And how would I know that liquor didn't go with his medication?"

Flora was sobbing again. In between gasps Jenny heard, "He wanted me to take it in my mouth, but I don't do that. There are some things I don't do, and that one's at the top of the list. I don't care how much he said he loved me."

"How'd you get him out?"

"He's crazy. He just went. Picked himself up, got dressed, and went. Right after I called you. Maybe he heard me calling. He said, 'Goodbye, Flora, you'll never see me again. You humiliated me, and I am not a man who puts up with humiliation.' Poor thing, he's mad about me."

Flora burst out laughing. In a second Jenny joined her.

"You should have heard him," Flora said, mimicking the stance and voice of an outraged male. "'I am not a man who puts up with humiliation,'" and went off into another peal of laughter.

"But why the gun? Why did he have a gun?" Jenny said.

"What a funny question. Lots of people in Miami carry guns. Mostly men, but women too. For safety. It's common practice. He had a jewelry store on Lincoln Road. You need a gun in that case. Would you like some frozen yogurt?" Flora was suddenly in a new mode. "I'm dying for real ice cream, aren't you, Jenny? But I've got some very good fat-free stuff."

They ate the smooth, cool cream with two chocolate Mallomars each.

"To hell with arteries and waistlines," Flora said. "I love Mallomars ever since I was a kid. Remember how poor we were, how hard Mama and Papa had to work in the little grocery store? No joke raising seven kids."

Jenny bit into a cookie and lost herself in her own memories of Mama and Papa. How distant and forbidding their disciplinary father had seemed when they were little, and how powerless and pitiful when he was old, how tender their mother always, scrubbing, cooking, bathing, and feeding with no thought for herself, wrapping every service to each of them in a packet of love.

"No joke raising me, for sure," Flora said, and reminded Jenny of a scary night when they were fourteen and nineteen years old and had picked up two grown men at a movie house. Or Flora had picked them up, with Jenny standing by, too frightened to get into their car on the offer of a ride home. Flora flounced in, calling Jenny a big baby. Jenny went home alone, so afraid that she cried all the way and sat on the apartment stoop waiting, numb with despair, sure that her sister was dead, or worse, as good as dead. When she had given up on ever seeing Flora again, the car came to a stop at the curb and Flora was ejected, sobbing. They had pawed her, torn buttons off her blouse, ripped off a stocking, and slapped her face when she bit them (Flora was a biter), but her shoes came flying out the door after her, and the stocking, and once they were safely upstairs it was clear that she wasn't badly hurt.

"It's your soul, your womanly soul they attack," Flora said, wrapping the Mallomar box in a plastic bag. "That's why we weep. That's why I wept then and why I weep now. They'll never understand.

Never. They think we have no right to a sex life, not even when we're young. If you want sex then you're bad, and now if you still want sex you're still bad, just because in their eyes you're old, and out of your mind as well."

"Who?" Jenny said.

"Men," said Flora vigorously, almost cheerful. "Men. Any man. Doctors especially. Men psychiatrists. The worst. Don't let a doctor know you're still passionate. At age eighty-five? Sex is a sin. It's proof that you're mad. If I called the cops, like you said, they'd put *me* away, not that crazy man I got rid of by the skin of my teeth." She began to cry again.

"Want more ice cream?" Jenny said.

"Would you have done it? Would you have done what he wanted me to do?"

"If I loved him," Jenny said.

"You mean you have?" Flora was astounded.

"When I loved them, or believed I did. If they asked."

"Did you like it?"

"I don't know. Who remembers the things you do in bed."

"In bed. You can't even talk sex. Fucking," Flora

said. "Call it fucking. And who is this 'they'? You always said you only loved one man."

"Well, I had two husbands, remember, and I thought I loved them both. I *did* love them both. Differently."

Flora laughed harshly. "You're hopeless. You have to make everything nice, smooth, beautiful, romantic. True love shit. You can't stand the idea of straight sex—lust, plain old lust. That's all it is, there ain't no true love." And after a pause, "Did both those bastards make you do that for them?"

"Hey," Jenny said lightly, "you're behind the times. Lots of people like oral sex. Nobody thinks anything of it anymore. Anything goes. And they weren't bastards."

"It's not a question of *think*. It's disgusting. Don't tell me that women enjoy that. You're lying. I bet you never did anything but lie under your man and let him come in you. You're just showing off, posing as a look-how-liberated-I-am female. And they *were* bastards if they made you do it, but I bet anything you're lying. Next thing you'll be claiming you've had abortions, just to be in with the times. I know you think that it's perfectly okay to kill."

"I never had an abortion. I had three births, deliberate, planned."

"Neither did I. I'm very proud of never having an abortion. Life is sacred. I hold life sacred. That's one thing. I never had an abortion."

"Come off it, Flora," Jenny said. She felt better, almost normal, and was answering Flora's arguments as she would anybody's. "Abortion is a lot better than an unwanted child. Talk about 'true love shit.' 'Life is sacred' is the real shit. How about war? How about the death penalty? Starvation and poverty?"

"No real woman with love in her heart could ever have an abortion. Don't argue oranges and lemons."

"How about Eva and Naomi? Eva had one abortion and Naomi had two. They're not real women with love in their hearts? They should have had seven children like Mama?"

"They never did," Flora shouted. "You're lying. You'd lie about anything to win an argument. And you dare to say Naomi had two abortions. Maybe, maybe, *maybe* she had one when she was having that affair with that insufferable shoe salesman. After all, she was only nineteen and didn't know any better. And then when she got pregnant he wouldn't marry her. But she never had two. Never."

"She did. She had two. After my first marriage, before I had kids, she came to stay with me after her second abortion, and I gave her a bacon and tomato sandwich and some good pea soup I had cooked up. Though I could hardly cook at all then. She told Mama she had caught a bad cold and would spend the weekend with me getting over it. It was between her two marriages, when she was screwing around with that painter she met at Lewisohn Stadium. He was very dark, and she suspected he was part black. So even though he wanted to marry her, she didn't want to, and who knows whether he really would have."

"Naomi was in love with that guy, and he wasn't part black, you just made that up to excuse her."

"I don't need to make up anything to excuse Eva and Naomi. I don't consider they committed any crime. And I didn't mean that part about him being black the way you took it."

"It's a crime. Abortion's a crime. Rabbi Shulman said so."

"Well, let Rabbi Shulman try having a baby at a terrible time in his life when he can't cope. Let him try it."

"Rabbi Shulman is a wonderful man nearly

ninety years old, Jenny, so show some respect. And you're telling me that Eva, safely married—because she had to be if you were old enough to know about it—that Eva chose to have an abortion instead of a baby?"

"That's what I'm telling you," Jenny said, worn out but dragging herself through the proof. "She left the kids for the weekend, and it turned out that what Eva said was poison ivy was really the measles the kids were sick with, but she couldn't tell Mama the truth, and we took care of them for her. We played checkers, slap the jack, and go fish till we were ready to drop. You remember. She came to pick them up looking so white and sick I was terrified for her. Mama said, 'What kind of weekend at the beach you come back paler than you went?' and Eva told her some cockamamie story about it raining the whole time. I thought they messed up some way, those awful doctors. Back then, they botched up horribly. I was sure she had been harmed. She looked awful."

Flora burst into tears. "All you remember are the bad things."

"Dammit, don't start crying again. That wasn't bad," Jenny pleaded. "We helped. We loved them.

We worried. It was dangerous, they had to have guts to do it, and we were good to them, both of us. We understood. You helped as much as I did."

"I don't remember any of that," Flora said.

"It doesn't matter," Jenny said. She was very tired.

"It does matter. You twist everything around. Now suddenly you're the broad-minded worldly person who knows all about sex, when you've always been a goody-good puritan disapproving of everything I did, jealous of all the men I had and acting superior about everything." Flora was working herself into a fury. "And another thing. You never had a man I didn't get for you. I introduced you to both your husbands. Without me you never even would have had a man." Then, fiercely, "When was the last time you had sex anyway?"

Jenny thought, *Why am I answering her?* "A long time ago. The year before Paul died. He was too sick that whole year before he died."

"For God's sake, Jenny, that was almost five years ago. You mean you haven't had sex in five years? And you dare to act as if I'm some kind of backward ignoramus and you're the liberated enlightened—"

Now it was Jenny who burst into tears and Flora who took Jenny in her arms and rocked her back and forth, soothing and smoothing, pledging over and over that she would never hurt Jenny again, saying, "Sorry sorry sorry," and then, "But what did I do, what did I say, I didn't mean anything, if I did do something wrong I didn't mean to, I love you, you came as soon as I called, I'll never forget that. There are only the two of us left now, let's help one another, Eva and Naomi are on the downslide, it's only a matter of time with them, soon there will only be us left, no one else to depend on but us, let's lean on one another."

"It's okay, I didn't mean to cry," Jenny answered. "I'm tired, I'm upset, we'll do better tomorrow. Time to go to bed now, call it a day. Let's call it a day."

4

MEMOIR PERFORMANCE!!!

The evening of the day of Naomi's operation, Jenny made the mistake of taking a bath instead of a shower. She had always loved baths, running the hot water until it foamed with good-smelling oily bubbles, resting there for a solid hour if it pleased her. And it did please her, even in the stained, too-small tub of her oceanfront room, until it came time to get up and out and she couldn't. Get up or get out. She couldn't. She couldn't haul her body up and out of the tub, which, as if cursed, had been transformed into a loathsome tomb holding her fast.

Grabbing the sides of the tub and pulling herself erect didn't work. Her body, the tub, the water were all too well oiled. She twisted, tried getting on one knee. She slipped and slid, hurting her back. She tried other positions, straining every muscle. Nothing worked. She would die in Miami after all, trapped in a bubble bath. She lay back, gathering strength, quieting her racing heart, forcing herself to think.

If she emptied the bath water, ran fresh water over herself and the tub? Worth a try. Removing all traces of the oil took a long time. Impatient, she made several attempts to pull herself up during the process, but couldn't. She laughed at the ridiculousness of her predicament, saw the scene as from the outside, then cried, sorry for this poor old body stuck in a bathtub. In a tremendous last-ditch effort she managed to kneel, and with another great effort stand up and miraculously step out of the tub. She felt as if she had won the lottery. Shaking, crying, laughing, she toweled, powdered, put on a gown, and got into bed, more exhausted than she had ever been in her life.

The day had been a mess. She had been alone in the mess, Flora busy with arrangements for her upcoming performance. Jenny had hired a medical van to get Naomi to the hospital, and once there, she had wheeled Naomi from station to station, filling out forms, endlessly waiting. The forms and the formalities completed, she wheeled her sister to a section of the hospital where Naomi was prepared for the operation by way of a long, mysterious process that took more than two hours, from which Jenny was excluded. Naomi described it to her later as mostly more waiting, though there had been some measuring, some X-raying, some marking of the groin.

Jenny waited. And waited. She waited in differently decorated locales, waited longest in a brilliantly green gardenlike room resembling a TV sitcom set. She leafed through magazines, reading a few lines of many different articles that blurred before her senses. Whether the journalists wrote of high events or low, the words all turned to nonsense in her head.

In between wheeling Naomi about and carrying papers and X-rays to various locations, she talked cheerful nonsense to ease Naomi's depressed panic. At last they arrived at what seemed to be the final waiting room, soberly done in brown and gold, filled with patients and their caretakers marking time in the dull air of preoperative tension. It was there that Jenny learned Naomi was in an outpatient operating facility where the ill were cut up, allowed to recover for a few hours in still another crowded waiting room, and then sent home. In the brochure this procedure was described as a great new innovation that did the patient much good.

Jenny threw a fit, causing consternation among the nurses, attendants, and clerks within a bustling enclosure at one end of the room. She threw it quietly, not to disturb Naomi or the other patients. Nobody outside the enclave paid attention. All those waiting inside seemed to be afflicted with a numb, sickly despair.

"She's ninety years old," Jenny repeated in a strong whisper. "She lives in a residence, in a room. Alone. She's alone. There's no way I'm going to take her back to her residence right after the operation. You're keeping her here, in the hospital, where she belongs, where she can be taken care of."

"It's not *right* after," a clerk said. "We keep them here for a number of hours until they're able to—"

"You're out of your mind," Jenny said. "She's ninety years old. You might as well tell her to get up out of her wheelchair and run around the block. I want to speak to her surgeon."

"We carefully explained the procedure to the patient, and gave her a brochure."

"Wonderful," Jenny said. "Tell the brochure to

take her back to her residence, because I won't. She needs to stay in the hospital after an operation. She's ninety years old."

It became Jenny's litany. She intoned it to more clerks, more nurses, then interns, anesthesiologists, doctors, and finally to Naomi's surgeon, a sixtyish handsome man, all charm and reassurance. Naomi would be kept in hospital care as long as needed. One night certainly, two or three if necessary. All this brouhaha Jenny managed out of hearing of Naomi, who complained of Jenny's desertion.

"I thought you came to be with *me* until I go under the knife. Where do you keep disappearing to? I know I'm a terrible bother, but please stay with me, Jenny, I'm really nervous. I know you love to talk to people, but please . . ."

Jenny stayed. She was given permission to stay through all the preliminaries, through the nurses' questions and routine examinations. She hung on through the move to a large open room like an emergency or intensive care division, she tied and retied Naomi's flowered hospital gown, she watched a nurse help Naomi into a gurney bed, she stayed and smoothed the covers. Naomi's serene, amazingly young head remained itself in this alienating setting, though her clear hazel eyes continued to plead. *Stay with me.* Jenny stayed. She held Naomi's hand, she made little jokes. One bed was empty. Five others were occupied by patients in varying stages of sedation. Doctors and nurses ran in and out. Little bells rang. Buzzers buzzed. Beepers beeped. Another long wait made Naomi fret. She was hot, cold, thirsty, dyspeptic, her legs ached, she had a stitch in her side, and from time to time she whimpered, "Don't let them hurt me, Jenny."

A breezy young nurse deftly set up an intravenous through Naomi's papery skin. A breezy young doctor joined the nurse, blocking Jenny's vision. Naomi accused Jenny when they left: "That hurt, they hurt me." Soon she was under sedation, rambling happily out of the hospital world into a warm place of love and laughter. She told an incomprehensible joke. She sang, "'It's a long road to Tipperary, it's a long road to home.'" She giggled and sang, "'Ain't misbehavin, I'm savin my love for you.'" She raised Jenny's hand to her lips and kissed Jenny's fingers. "My baby sister, my dear baby sister." She was smiling, happy. Jenny kissed her on her fine, clear forehead.

There was no place for Jenny to sit, but she

thought she'd better not create another disturbance by requesting a chair. As long as they let her stay. She stood. Her legs ached. Her feet burned. She stayed. Naomi fell asleep. Jenny considered searching for a comfortable chair, a toilet, a cup of coffee, but what if Naomi woke to find her gone? She stayed. Naomi did wake when she was wheeled away, woke to smile and reach out a hand to Jenny to come with her, but Jenny was briskly told to wait in the outer room; it would be a matter of a few hours, the surgeon would come to speak to her after the operation. And then, more kindly, by the same breezy nurse, she was urged to relax, get something to eat, take a little walk, not to worry.

It was too hot to walk very far. She meandered along the paths of the huge complex of structures, walkways, parking lots, building names, the Sol and Minnie Rosenblatt Center for Psychological Disorders, the George P. Isserman Eye and Ear Institute, the Florence Cohen Brown Dentistry Center, in and out of the shade, dizzy from the heat and anxiety for Naomi, among plantings of deep green shrubs and banks of impatiens. It was a little like getting lost in the Maine woods, where the massive tree you've just encountered looks a lot like the one you left behind some time ago, and is in fact the same. All medical buildings loomed alike, whatever the donors' names attached.

Impatiens everywhere. Jenny loved impatiens, used it herself in her window boxes at home, but was learning to loathe the innocent blossoms in Miami. Odd that it was called both impatiens and patience— or had she got that wrong, along with her other late, faulty knowledge of the botanical world? She found herself turned around, directionless, in a blazing hot parking lot where an American black man and a Latino were having a repetitive two-sentence dispute.

The black man had his hand on the door of an aged Mercedes Benz in excellent shape. "I heard what you said," he shouted. "I know what you meant." He was large, bearded, bald, dressed in pressed chinos and a white top that said "Tommy" in large blue letters in front and "Hilfiger" in large black letters in back. "I heard what you said. I know what you meant."

The Latino, equally large but smooth-faced, wore blue jeans and a navy blue cotton V-neck that said "Syracuse" in white stitching across the center of a large orange-and-white S. "Wad I say? Wad?

Wad I say?" His wife, or girlfriend, a pretty young woman in shorts and a yellow flounce-collared top that said "Romantique" in a wavering script of pale multicolors, wasn't paying any attention to the exchange, though her guy kept appealing to her as much as to the black man, throwing out his arms and putting on a face of exaggerated innocence. "Wad I say? Wad?"

Jenny moved on into the shade of the nearest building and ducked inside. She had entered the very heart of the medical industry, the general hospital. The lobby was alive with activity, as crowded and noisy as an airport. She breathed easier in the cool of the air conditioning and managed to claim one of the black Naugahyde attached-to-one-another chairs that had emptied at that moment. Surely in this place of business there must be a satisfactory lavatory and cafeteria, perhaps even an upholstered chair with arms. She rested in the bustle of moving bodies, beepers, loud talk, announcements. Somewhere in this industrial complex Naomi's life was being saved or ended or prolonged into intervals of better and worse while the immense machinery of health care went about its lucrative business. Jenny hoisted herself laboriously to her feet. Ladies' room. Cafeteria.

To pee. To comb her hair. To eat. To keep going.

The ladies' room was fine, clean and properly stocked, but the cafeteria was overwhelming, an enormous space, entered through the serving area, redolent with warring food smells. Overflowing bread baskets, overflowing salad bar, fresh fruit bar, freshly made sandwich section, hot food—Cuban, Chinese, Southern fried chicken, vegetarian, pasta with varied sauces—low-fat low-salt health stuff, refrigerated cases of desserts, juices, sodas, tables of hot coffee and tea, regular, decaffeinated, and herbal. In a nostalgic rush of longing for her dead husband, Jenny joined the Cuban line, waiting her turn to order a meal she couldn't finish, could hardly begin on, actually, when after negotiating the long lines of receiving and paying and beverage getting she finally seated herself in the huge dining area and studied her plate: Cuban thin steak covered with wilted onions on a bed of shredded lettuce, white rice and black beans, side of *plátanos maduras*, and the white melon-textured vegetable whose name she had forgotten but had requested from the server by pointing. The food conjures up her husband, young, grinning at her, teasing. "You're going to eat all that? Never." A young Jenny smiles too.

"Don't rush me. Pig. You'll get the leftovers when I finish."

She ate a few bites. Delicious. But hard to swallow. The noise in the great crowded room had a life of its own, a low roaring presence. Among interns, nurses, technicians, clerks, patients, visitors, children running, crying, moody and silent, she sat alone at a corner of a long, fully occupied table, her eyes unwillingly concentrated on the sad silent children, worrying for them, for their tenderness and their toughness, for their survival, while torturing her brain to remember the name of the white vegetable. It had been steamed, then lightly sprinkled with olive oil and delicate slivers of garlic. Delicious. Just the way Abuela cooked it.

Yucca. Or *malanga.* Happiness, victory, success suffused her being. She had recalled a name. Two names, actually. Well, close enough.

She emptied her almost full tray in the trash container. A meal. The city of Sarajevo could feed for a day on the amount of food circulated in this cafeteria. A sudden smell of fresh dill brought back her own mother alive in her kitchen. Dill in the Friday night chicken soup. "Eat, eat, think of the starving Armenians." The mothers, the dead mothers, once alive in their kitchens, a generation of mothers—gone for good. *Yes*, she thought, *for good. The old ways are dead and gone. Forget them. There is only the dangerous present, where we have to figure out some way to live together and die together.*

She concentrated on finding her way back through the wilderness of buildings to the dull brown and gold room where she waited and waited and waited for Naomi's handsome surgeon to come and lie to her about how long and in what shape Naomi would live until she died.

"Don't you dare let her come here to entertain," Eva said.

"Me?" Jenny raised her eyebrows. "I have nothing to do with it. She's on this entertainment roster that services senior centers, retirement centers, nursing homes. That's what she told me. I've never seen her perform, have you?"

"Yes, God help me. I'll be embarrassed to death if she shows up here. Though there are always people who think she's terrific—the kind of people who think Howard Stern is terrific. Well, like the other night. You saw how some of them thought she was so wonderful. Isn't that incredible? Wasn't that something? My poor granddaughter, she was embarrassed to death. She is such an angel, she didn't fuss about it at all. She just laughed." And Eva laughed, a gay young laugh, as if in imitation.

They were seated in the shade of the awnings outside the dining room at Eva's residence, close to the swimming pool, empty at this early morning hour. Eva was neatly put together, as usual, though her hair looked a little funny. The hairdresser had left a hole with pink scalp showing through the thin white strands. Eva had been taken off the steroid that ballooned her face, which in this new incarnation was so thin that nose and ears looked enormous. Jenny remembered an item in de Beauvoir's *The Coming of Age*. It seemed that the ears continued to grow as long as one lived. Perhaps even in the grave, like hair and nails?

"Maybe it's because we're sisters and can't really appreciate one another," Jenny said, thinking more about herself than about Flora. "Because she's different, we . . ."

"I'll say she's different. God spare me. Wait till you hear that poem of hers she reads about the sexy grandma. She throws in all those words, clitoris, penis, orgasm. She doesn't care what she says." Eva shook her head in disbelief. "And the audience eats it up."

She looked hard at Jenny and took her hand in the still-strong grip of her long, elegantly manicured fingers. Jenny noted that she had covered her liver spots with makeup.

"No, not at all, Jenny. We appreciate you. We know that what you do isn't a trick. She's all tricks. You're genuine. We're all proud of you. Even Flora, even though she's jealous, she can't help being proud, you should hear how she talks you up to other people when you're not around. But that's enough about Flora anyway. What about you? What are you doing now? How are things going? What are you working on? I loved that article you did in the *New York Times* about Emerson being Jewish—not really Jewish, you know what I mean, the way you linked him up with the Talmud, that was terrific. But how is everything, how are you getting along? Do you need money? Are you managing okay? I'm sure your children are always a comfort. How are they? How are they all? I'm so glad you came down, it was so good for Naomi to have you there with her, it's so good to see you. It's so hard, with Mama and Papa gone, and the boys, the boys all gone, it's so good that you're here, little Jenny, little sister Jenny. Whatever your accomplishments, you're always my baby sister, God bless you, it's wonderful to be with you."

And wonderful for Jenny to be with an Eva restored to her usual self. A kind of peaceful content Jenny rarely experienced loosened her guarded speech. She talked about herself; she babbled; she didn't worry about what she was saying or how she was saying it; she relaxed in the warm bath of Eva's love and emerged ready for the ordeal of Flora's show that afternoon.

Flora called the show "MEMOIR PERFOR-MANCE!!!" With three exclamation marks. She had had flyers xeroxed, and with Jenny's help she had tacked them up in the lobby of the Hebrew Home for the Aged, Miami Beach's oldest Jewish nursing home, in South Beach. It was not in the heart of the trendy new international hot spot, "where the action is," but Ocean Drive was near enough.

The residents arrived in the lounge full of lunch and mostly sleepy (with a few obstreperous exceptions), men and women in varying stages of infirmity, massed in wavering rows of folding chairs inter-

spersed with wheelchairs, gurneys, walkers, canes.
Women predominated, ten to one. There was an
overexcited buzz in the room, a chaotic hum of
meaningless noise, as in Bellevue, where Jenny had
once visited a friend, and Sing Sing, where she had
taught a literature course in the sixties.

Flora was decked out in gold-toned purple for
the occasion: purple skirt, gold lamé tailored shirt,
gold-lapelled purple jacket, lamé baseball cap on
shoe-black curly hair, gold lamé stockings, gold kid
pumps, big gold calf bag, purple eyeshadow, coal-
black eyeliner. There was no stage, just a little podium, a mike, and a piano off to the side. A harsh
spotlight shone directly on Flora's face, though the
room was bright with sun. Heavy makeup and explo-
sive energy made her seem younger than her eighty-
five years; she might have passed for early seventies,
late sixties.

To prolonged applause, Flora was introduced by
the aged, lively male director of activities in a
marked New York Jewish singsong. Flora had apparently decided to enhance her glamour by having
him mention Jenny, whom he described as "the
well-known professional writer sister of the star of
the occasion, a woman with so many accomplish-

ments it would take me half a day to recite them, a professor, a lecturer, a writer . . ." At the close of his remarks, when he asked Jenny to rise, she nodded her head, gesturing toward Flora as the *one* star of the occasion, and sat down quickly, ignoring the continuing applause. The audience liked to clap hands. It gave them something to do.

A man seated nearby was thrilled by Jenny's presence, going on about his son, "a noted professor at the University of Illinois. Surely you know Professor Meyer Asher? Very well known, very well thought of." She nodded, smiled, frowned, put her finger to her lips, pointed meaningfully at Flora, who was struggling to be heard over the general din. A woman whose entirely wrinkled face was lit up with delight approached slowly with the help of her three-footed walker, clearly eager to talk to Jenny, but the activities director intervened, determinedly seated her, and commanded the audience to quiet down. The excited rustling subsided somewhat.

Flora began with a joke. Jenny was so tense, so convinced that Flora was headed for total disaster, that she understood nothing of the content. The activities director led the laughter and applause, and the audience joined in enthusiastically, those who were still awake. The room was hot and airless, and there was a low hum of rasping breath. Here and there someone snored.

Flora proceeded with her multimedia memoir: the story of her life through anecdote, poetry, a display of blown-up family photographs, a couple of songs, a little waltzy parody dancing, and some piano playing, random bits of Mozart, Bach, Beethoven, Satie. Slowly Jenny calmed down enough to hear. The fact was that Flora was dazzling in an egocentric, crazy, contemporary way. If Flora weren't her sister, if the performance were a stranger's, it would have started buzz words rolling around in Jenny's head: deconstructionist, postmodernist, feminist. But Flora *was* her sister, and it was all Jenny could do to keep herself from fleeing the room. She stayed. She stayed with her heart pounding, recoiling when she wasn't laughing, hating what she heard when she wasn't lost in admiration of its daring.

She was jarred into recognition of a direct quote, without attribution, of a complete sentence from a memoir she herself had published. And another, from Elinor Wylie, also without attribution. Were there other borrowings she hadn't caught? Was it all simply stolen? Then she found herself laughing aloud as Flora told a story about failing the Papp Test—when her act was rejected by the Public Theater's founder. That joke was original, or if it wasn't, Jenny had never heard it before.

Imperceptibly, as the one-hour show continued, the fretful hum in the room rose, and when Flora segued from a poem she had written about Mama into the singing of "My Yiddishe Mama," a woman square in the middle of the audience stood and joined her, caterwauling in a high moan, keeping a sort of time with Flora, jerking her arthritic body back and forth and side to side to the rhythm—*hmmm, hmmm, hmmm, hmmm*—while other voices took up the *hmmm, hmmm* in a demented backup chorus.

In her dashes from mike to piano to floor to mike, Flora had torn off her lamé cap and the purple jacket, but she was still very flushed, a film of sweat on her throat, her curly black hair gone lank. Yet her eyes glowed and her voice stayed true and strong even as the audience accompaniment threatened to swamp the act.

Jenny was appalled. She wanted to rescue Flora, pull her from her self-imposed punishment at the podium. Flora needed no rescuing. She challenged her overstimulated hearers like a winning boxer, hands on hips, head thrown back, joy in all her bearing.

"Well, my friends, would you care to come up here and share my mike with me, or could you give me the courtesy of some silence and some attention? Well, do I hear an answer? I'm not continuing until I have silence."

The director helped her again. In his deepest tones he demanded "respect for the artiste entertainer of the day. Come on now, you know better, you know how to behave, let's show our respect for our most unusual artiste entertainer." He was walking toward the giddy leader of this ego insurrection, shushing and shaking his finger at her, pushing her into a chair, when yet another disturbance erupted. A woman with a broken leg trussed up in an elevated cast was being hastily wheeled out by her nurse. The face of the patient was a strange blue color, and her breathing was noisy. The room quieted.

Flora elaborately thanked the audience, then worked the woman on the gurney into her act, throwing out her arms, pleading in an Al Jolson parody. "Mamele, Mamele, my little Mamele, don't go, stay with me, I'm good, I'm good, and at my worst I'm not that bad, am I, friends?" The director once again led the laughter and applause, which he tried to steer into an end to the presentation, but Flora outwitted him and sang one last song in a mix of English and Yiddish, bringing her show to a smash conclusion.

Getting out of the home was an impeded advance through infirm admirers, Jenny trailing Flora as she graciously accepted compliments. Once outside, they walked slowly through the heat to Flora's favorite Italian restaurant, a few blocks away on what Flora always called Fabulous Ocean Drive, as if the adjective were part of its formal name. There had been no time for them to lunch beforehand. Anyway, Flora preferred to perform on an empty stomach. "We actors never eat before a show."

They were seated outdoors in an area spottily shaded by a beautiful tree Jenny couldn't identify, at a big round table all of whose extra chairs Flora swallowed up. She placed her jacket and lamé cap on one and her oversized gold bag on another, kicking off her gold pumps to put her feet up on the only chair left. Then she peeled off her lamé stockings, undid the top three buttons of her shirt, closed her eyes, opened her mouth wide, and breathed deeply.

"I'm exhausted. I must have a drink. And I don't mean water." She laughed her boisterous laugh.

A busboy had set up menus, flatware, cloth napkins, large stemmed glasses of ice water topped with a slice of lime.

"Where's our waiter?" Flora's voice was still the large voice of the actress. "I want a Bloody Mary with a big stick of celery. They do that great here, with a smitch of horseradish."

"This is on me," Jenny said. "After-performance celebration."

"In that case I'll have another Bloody Mary when I've finished the first one."

"The sky's the limit."

"Not that you've said a word about my performance. Not that I care. I had enough admirers all over me to satisfy anybody."

She had indeed been showered with extravagant praise after her show. Did it matter to her that adoration had dribbled out of the mouths of stuttering stroke victims advancing through a thicket of canes, crutches, walkers, and wheelchairs? Was it the crippled source that left her dissatisfied? Or was there never enough praise of any kind? Jenny's quick kiss and murmur of "wonderful, wonderful" obviously hadn't satisfied.

"It was amazing," Jenny said. "Just wonderful."

"You hated it." Flora turned aside to stop a waiter and order her drink. "The trouble with you," she resumed, "is that you're thoroughly corrupted by the New York scene. You think New York is all that matters, Broadway is all that matters. You have no conception of the breadth of senior events, wherever they take place. I've done dozens of them, and believe me, a senior event is just as important as an off-off-Broadway show. Did you know I won first place here in Miami in a worst poetry contest? In your book," she said, talking through the arrival of her Bloody Mary, stirring vigorously with the full-leafed celery stalk, taking a long drink, half choking as she swallowed, "in your book that would be a disgrace, in my book it's a triumph. Did you ever hear of Allen Ginsberg? That man is a *poet*, not the kind of dried-up academic poet you're always quoting and raving about. You don't know anything about poetry. *He* said *I* was a terrific poet. Where's your drink? Aren't you having anything?"

Jenny said, "Water's fine for me now. I'll have a glass of red wine with lunch," quickly adding, "I'm the first to admit I know very little about poetry, Flora, but I love Allen Ginsberg, and if he said . . ."

"Well, that's a relief, hearing you admit you're wrong about something." Flora drained half of her oversized glass.

Jenny sipped at her water, mentally withdrew from what was a no-win conversation, and immersed herself in her surroundings and the constant parade on the sidewalk. The restaurants that lined Ocean Drive were housed in restored 1920s Art Deco hotels. Here camp was king. Queen, Jenny corrected herself. Their facades were embellished in unusual hues—pinks, greens, all shades of Flora's purples—along with the more usual gray, white, and black. Some were as lavish in design and color as oriental palaces. From the ocean, some distance beyond the stretch of avenue and then of park, of coconut palms and wide sandy beach, the sea breeze battled with emissions from the expensive cars cruising by and the food smells from the posh restaurants. Parked at the curb, an antique Rolls-Royce, exquisitely maintained, brought passersby to a halt to admire its splendid brass fixtures, but most quickly moved on. Strollers on Ocean Drive were not there to see but to be seen.

And they were something to see. Hair of all natural and unnatural colors and cuts, no hair at all or hair all over the place, eyes sunglassed, naked of makeup, or wildly made up, bared asses bosoms bellybuttons, bare backs, bare middles, bare legs legs legs, bare feet arms underarms crotches. High-fashion bare, though in a pinch bare alone would do it. Thonged bare asses in abundance, men's and women's, painted bodies and pierced parts, tiny underwear dresses, long clinging shifts with nothing underneath, soft soft pants displaying the penis and the mound, many no-tops and microscopic bras. If cover-up clothes were worn, they were expensive baggy raggedy limp, with their wearers carrying backpacks or sporty duffels slamming around their sloppy pants legs. The film crowd.

"Fantastic," Jenny said, hoping for a change of subject. She waved in the direction of a middle-aged hunk, naked except for tall cowboy boots, a cowboy hat, and a brilliant red scarf wrapped around his groin. Bright golden hair covered his body. Dyed? "Look at that one."

Flora barely glanced up. "Gay," she said. "That's the trouble. Hard to find a real man these days. But you probably wouldn't know what to do with him if you found one," she added, and without a pause, "I don't know what to order. Could we share some baked clams oreganato with our drinks? You know, I think I forgot to take my medication this morning. Now it's too late. It's a no-no with liquor."

"Sure," Jenny said, and flagged down a waiter. "Are you ready to order your main dish? What do you take? And what's it for?"

Flora waved away the question as the waiter arrived. "You see," she said after ordering another Bloody Mary, spaghetti with red clam sauce, and a green salad, "what you don't understand is how important the senior scene is down here in South Beach. You think that a senior event in South Beach is of no importance." Jenny heard the words italicized. *Senior scene. A senior event.*

"No, no," she said. "South Beach is very chic, everybody knows that. It's one of the chic places of the world. Right up there with the Via Veneto."

"Glad to hear it from your mouth," Flora said, and suggested that a half-carafe of red wine would be nice with their entrees.

When their orders arrived, Flora became more disheveled with every sip. She had pulled her skirt up high on her thighs, her white cotton brassiere showed above the opened lamé shirt, and she lolled on the chair as if the bones in her body had melted; there was a lot of rolling flesh exposed. The loud rock music had been changed to a Sinatra tape. She sang along: "If you are among the very young at heart."

A passing group of strollers called out, "Yeah, yeah, yeah, Grandma!"

"Grandma, yourself," Flora yelled, and gave them the middle finger.

They enjoyed that even more. An extraordinarily tall young woman in thick platform shoes that increased her height, with a thriving mane of black black hair, her perfect ass in a thong and her inflated breasts in a tiny lace bra revealing pale ivory skin, as if wind and sun never existed, detached herself from the group. With a deep bow and a dazzling smile, she laid a long-stemmed red rose on Flora's exposed pink thighs.

"Go, go, go," she intoned in a blessing.

"See?" Flora said. "You have to admit it, *schvester*, I'm a smash in South Beach."

5

HOME

By mid-spring some decisions had been reached. Eva and Naomi were headed for the same nursing home, expensive, reputedly very good—so long as the two stayed well enough and sane enough to avoid assignation to the dreaded third floor, where the dying messy crazies were housed. There had been endless conferences on the matter.

Flora was opposed, not to the place, which no one had seen yet, but to the concept of Eva and Naomi under the same roof.

"They don't get along, they've never gotten along. Naomi can't even stand Eva's wardrobe, she's always complaining that all Eva wears is pants. How can they see each other every day? What if they have to share the same closet? It's impossible."

Eva's children were in favor. They felt their mother would have more company and their burden would be eased. And they thought it would be nice if there were only one place for the family to visit.

"Killing two birds with one stone," Naomi had said, letting her bitterness show.

"Don't you like the idea?" Jenny said.

"What's to like?" She waved a hand, wiping it all away. "Doesn't matter, it's a big place, and it's not as if we're sharing a room. I guess it's a good idea. It will save all of you a lot of trouble."

"Don't worry about us. Think of yourself, what you want."

Naomi laughed. "Ah, what I want." She closed her eyes against further discussion. "Let it be, it's fine, it's fine."

Did Naomi understand that she was dying? The surgeon had recommended still another operation on the groin; the oncologist urged chemo, in addition or instead, to extend her life. How long? Hard to say, perhaps some months.

Naomi refused. "I just want to be left alone. No more tinkering. Just make sure they keep me out of pain, Jenny."

Jenny had asked the doctors how long Naomi might live without medical intervention. Again they found it hard to say. "Three months, with luck six or seven, difficult to predict," and as an afterthought, "or she could go any day."

Nobody was predicting the date of Eva's death. With the change of medication she seemed to be feeling very well. She was looking well too, and not so fretful, and she was content with the idea of the nursing home. Naomi's presence was an irrelevance since they wouldn't be right on top of one another. It couldn't be too bad, and if it turned out to be good, so much the better.

"We were never really close," Eva told Jenny. "You know that. All those old rivalries. Papa loved me best. Mama loved her best. I wanted it the other way around, and so did she. She was always prettier. I was jealous of that. And she was jealous of me—God knows why, I don't. Maybe because of my children and my grandchildren and the great-grandchildren. She messed up her life, and she has nobody but herself to blame. I'm sorry for her. She has nobody."

She has me, Jenny thought.

"She has you, thank God, she's lucky there, and she thinks the world of you, so she'll listen to you. She doesn't think much of me, but that's okay, I don't think much of her, and she'd never listen to anything I suggest. She listens to Flora, though, who can be depended on to steer her wrong."

"That's not true. You love one another. You know you do."

"Of course we love one another. We're sisters. That's why it's okay to be in the same nursing home. Even if it turns out bad, which I sincerely hope it won't."

"Eva, isn't it funny how we each think like that?"

"Like what?"

"That our sisters don't think much of us, that our family, you know, doesn't appreciate us, doesn't recognize, you know, our reality, the persons we really are . . ."

"I think the world of you, Jenny, you know that."

"Yes, but you know what I mean, what we're always saying about one another . . ."

"That's the way sisters are," Eva said. "We each want to be perfect, and we want all of us to be perfect. And we all want to be the favorite. Of everybody. We've all hurt one another. We've all messed up one way or another. But it doesn't matter anymore, Jenny, we're too old for that nonsense, who loves who the most, who's better, who's best, you, me, Flora, Naomi. We're all good enough."

"Good enough?" Flora was outraged by Jenny's

flawed attempt later to convey the conversation with Eva. "I'm the best, none of this second-rate 'good enough.' If Eva thinks she's good enough, that's her privilege, but I'm the best and so are you and so is Naomi in her way. I resent that. I really resent that. Trying to bring us all down to her level. She wallows in being normal. It's disgusting."

Jenny blamed herself for the outburst. She never should have opened up this can of worms for Flora's interpretation, especially since they faced an enormous task that would take as much diplomacy as the two of them could muster. With all the arrangements set, it was Jenny and Flora's job to see their sisters through the actual move.

More Jenny's job than Flora's, as it turned out. Flora had altered, as if she had stepped into another room by passing through her eighty-sixth birthday a few weeks earlier. Stepped into a permanent bedroom. Now she spent most of the day lying down, watching TV, dozing off, getting up to pee, roaming the living room, wandering into the kitchen, gazing into the refrigerator, eating a little snack, pacing the bedroom, lying down again, watching TV, dozing off, waking to pee . . . Jenny would force Flora to dress, then walk her, as she leaned heavily on

Jenny's arm, to the places she loved, McDonald's for their packaged apple pie and coffee in the afternoon, Wendy's for a chicken sandwich for supper.

Jenny made Flora attend a cookout on the broad terrace of her condominium, where she pushed and shoved alongside the other anxious Jewish and Latino residents to get her legitimate share of hotdogs with sauerkraut, cold cuts and coleslaw, and thick wedges of strawberry shortcake. A small but heated culture war was raging in the condominium. The Latinos wanted their food, and had victoriously achieved a separate smaller area where chicken and rice, black beans and *plátanos* were being served, to much whispered grumbling from the Jewish section. Jenny tried a little of each, alienating all sides.

In this controversy Flora came alive.

"What's wrong with people? Why can't they live and let live? Everybody pay their five dollars apiece and eat whatever they like. Hotdogs, fried bananas, who cares? Pay your five dollars and get your share. Their music, our music, who cares? Music's music."

Flora's position was an astonishment to Jenny. Impossible to predict her point of view on any subject.

"I paid my five dollars just like everybody else,"

Flora went on. "So did you. See that you get your share. You want fried bananas, why not? Everybody to her own taste. I hate fried bananas. There's chocolate macaroons on the dessert table too. Left over from Passover, I bet, but they can stay pretty fresh. Bring me a couple of those when you get us coffee."

For an hour and a half on the broad, warring, multilingual multicultural deck, Flora was her old onstage self, singing "Ruzinkas mit Mandlin" and "Amapola" without prejudice and to much applause before she collapsed into bed and stayed there, fixed before the TV, dozing, rising only to pee, pace the living room, stare into the refrigerator . . .

Jenny had taken a sublet in Flora's condominium, on another floor but near enough to be on call. Although it was more spacious and comfortable than the shabby beach hotel, Jenny found it harder to live in this intimate space the owners had created. Souvenirs made of shells. Shmeary abstract paintings. A complete maple bedroom set. Photographs of relatives on every surface. She tiptoed around, an unwelcome alien, creating a spot for herself before the oversized TV, where she took her hurried meals on a small folding table and quickly erased all signs of her intruder presence when she was finished.

She spent most of her time with her sisters, trying to keep Flora active, preparing Eva and Naomi for their moves to the nursing home. Eva's children had located the place by long distance, but it had been left to Jenny and Flora to inspect it. Flora begged off and sent Jenny on her own to "case the joint," as Flora put it.

"You've got to do it, Jenny. I'm no good anymore. I'm losing my marbles. Those places scare me so much I don't know shit from shinola. I wouldn't even know what questions to ask, and if I did I'd promptly forget the answers."

The home was a nondenominational Catholic nursing facility far from the beach but on an inland waterway dotted with boats and birds of infinite variety, a brilliant blue road bordered by flowering plants, playfully shaped skyscraper apartment houses and luxury hotels, the looming, looping white structures of the thruway in the distance, the whole lit in greens, blues, soft reds, like a stage set. The building itself was a dull square of red brick, but the grounds were lavish with patios festooned in striped awnings, round tables with matching striped umbrellas, and canvas chairs set out on tiled oases surrounded by greenery and blossoms.

Inside, the home made a failing effort to be homey. It was too big for that, too much like a hospital, the halls too long, too smelling of disinfectant, the tones too determinedly cheerful and loud, on the assumption that the patients were deaf and childish, as many were. There were nuns in slacks and dresses—no habits visible—and patients of all colors and backgrounds. Women, as usual, predominated. A rabbi and a priest were available for the religious, and there were regular services. Staff included a Jewish social worker, an Irish cashier, a Jewish handicapped man at the main desk, black nurses, attendants, aides, technicians, kitchen and cleaning help, men and women, Caribbeans and Latinos. The doctors were mainly white, as was administration, with an occasional black and Asian.

Eva's children had chosen a private room for her, sight unseen. Jenny was shown not *the* room Eva would occupy but one just like it. It was large, airy, located on the preferred second floor overlooking one of the gardens, big closet, private bath, armchair, TV mounted on one wall, crucifix on the other. (Good thing Flora hadn't come after all.)

Cost? Realistically, between six and seven thousand a month.

"What happens when her money's all gone?"

Eva's children were in charge of Eva's money, but Jenny was managing Naomi's.

"The patient is shifted to a Medicaid bed in a double room, the same as the room I'm about to show you for your other sister."

The young woman escorting Jenny was pretty, nicely put together in a black silk pantsuit lightened by a long string of gray-and-white beads made of some kind of tropical seed. She was essentially a saleswoman, but her spiel was heavily shmaltzed with compassionate phrasing: *caring, loving, close, family.* Her light blue eyes remained dead.

Naomi's room would be the same size on the same preferred floor, but with two beds separated by rings of curtain, two dressers, two armchairs, two big closets, two TVs, one bathroom, one large window overlooking a parking lot, one mounted crucifix. Cost? Four to five thousand. The bed, Jenny was assured, was assigned to Medicaid, no need to move the patient when her money gave out. Naomi's roommate-to-be was already a Medicaid patient, a sweet-faced blond woman who sat fully dressed in

her armchair in the darkest corner of the room, star-
ing and smiling. Though she looked younger, she
was ninety-four. She opened her arms to Jenny and
broadened her vague smile.

"She thinks you're her visitor. She never gets
any, poor thing."

Jenny blew her a kiss to no response and hurried
after the young woman, who was now showing her
the special rooms: for being bathed (terrifyingly
deep metal tubs like torture chambers), for being
exercised (machines and pads, less scary), and a sort
of classroom (one bookcase, a scattering of books,
pamphlets, and xeroxed sheets, a blackboard, a TV,
a computer).

Jenny had already visited the central lobby, fea-
turing exotic birds in a large glass enclosure with a
small flowering tree. Shut-in birds for shut-in
patients. A lunchroom off the lobby served ambulant residents: tablecloths, cloth napkins, fresh flowers in skinny vases, cafeteria aroma of clashing
foods. Naomi liked eating at a table set with cloth
and flowers. She'd hate the smell.

"But what if she can't manage a tray?"

"She can be waited on, or helped in any other
way. We have some wonderful volunteers."

Then on to a lounge where the ambulant on their own frail legs gathered with those using wheel-chairs, recliners, crutches, walkers, and canes. A heavy woman, garishly made up and obviously wigged, decked out in a sequined pantsuit, was per-forming a concert of golden oldies with a scratchy recording for backup. "Borsht Belt has-been," Flora called the type. Exhausted and out of breath, Has-been was winding up with "Bei Mir Bist Du Schoen." Ice cream and cookies next, the real draw of the per-formance. Jenny was offered a dish, and not know-ing how to refuse her escort without insult, she tried a mouthful. It was real ice cream, none of that low-fat yogurt stuff. She ate it greedily.

Eager to leave her, the saleswoman smiled, asked if Jenny had any other questions, pointed to the exit, and urged Jenny to visit the patio on her way out. Suddenly alive in all her body, she shook hands vigorously, assured Jenny that her sisters would be very happy at Serenity Villa, and bolted from the disheveled room of dying bodies.

Jenny sat for a minute. Across what passed for an aisle in that mess of furniture for the sick and dying, a slim, handsome man with a full head of white hair and a deeply tanned face had finished his ice cream. He was propped up in an elaborately fitted upholstered recliner on wheels, carefully dressed in expensive chinos and a Brooks Brothers striped dress shirt, the collar open and the long sleeves dashingly folded back below his elbows. One of the volunteers, a soft young woman in a long flowered dress, was trying to collect the refuse of his snack. He relinquished his paper plate but held on to his paper napkin. He seemed to have had a stroke. He couldn't speak. His dramatic dark eyes were eloquent. The young woman pressed him to drop the napkin into the black plastic garbage bag she carried, but he clutched it tighter the more she insisted.

"Would you like more ice cream, Mr. Kaplan? Is that it?"

He couldn't respond. His eyes glowed with a mysterious message. The young woman tugged at the napkin. He tightened his grip, she tugged, he gripped harder. The young woman gave up with a little shrug of incomprehension.

"That's okay, Mr. Kaplan. We'll get it later."

The urgency in his eyes changed when the volunteer left. Jenny watched him concentrate on the napkin, fixing it with an evident emotion as strong as lust or love, until the fingers loosened and dropped it in his lap, revealing two squashed cookies which he labored to bring up to his mouth to chew with slow, victorious satisfaction. When he had swallowed the last crumb, he put back his head and closed the lids on his lustrous eyes.

On her way out through the patio, she passed a black family visiting a paralyzed old man in another recliner on wheels. She sat down on a bench in the shade and watched. They were a large family, one very old couple, many middle-aged and young people, children, babies, and a big golden-haired dog who kept his long-nosed noble head in the old man's lap. They laughed and talked, horsed around, chased down the wandering babies. They ate and drank sodas, fruits, nuts, chocolates, ice cream, and hunks of birthday cake, the bigger kids racing around the damp paths of the recently watered garden, a daughter son grandson granddaughter taking turns at the side of the recliner, patting the dog's head to keep him put, smoothing the old man's round wrinkled forehead and his thin white hair, kissing hugging holding up the babies for him to see, urging the playing children to stop by for a minute to say hello to Grandpa, Great-grandpa, stroking stroking smiling smiling smiling into the old man's eyes hazed over with immobilized love and pain and happiness.

She had neglected to call a cab from the desk of the nursing home. Stuck in an area where taxis didn't cruise, she headed for the bus stop but halted some way from its shaded bench. A homeless man had made it his library/office. Instead of a shopping cart full of rags, his was packed with books, pads, manuscripts. There was a suitcase strapped to the side of the cart, probably holding his clothing. He was neatly dressed, washed and combed, though very hairy: long full beard, a huge halo of hair tied into a ponytail with a shoelace, hairy arms and feathery hairs on the backs of his hands and fingers down to the nails.

She wanted to talk to him, ask what he was working on, but he was too intent to disturb. He was writing in a script so tiny it was barely legible, though she strained hard to read the words flowing on long lined sheets of yellow paper held by a clipboard—a method of working so like her own it startled her. He was even using one of her favorite pens, a heavy silver Waterman. He had a lean, worn face. His concentration in this public corner of the covered bus stop was exemplary, a lesson in ignoring the nonessential. He was oblivious to Jenny's hungry curiosity and to the presence of the other waiting passengers, who gave him a wide berth. He worked as if he were entirely alone. He searched out a book from the shopping cart, whirled pages, found what he needed, wrote rapidly in the tiny script. Heat, breeze, insects were nothing to him, nor the ceaseless traffic whizzing by, nor the incongruity of a poster behind his head of four young women in wet-lipped hilarity cavorting in scanty costumes and selling—what? Makeup, hair dye, underwear, sportswear, bathing suits, evening gowns, shoes? Impossible to say if one didn't recognize the logo, as she did not.

She envied him. What was wrong with her? She was actually envying a homeless, crazy bum. Because he was working.

She couldn't work in Miami. There was nothing of substance left in her head after visiting Naomi and Eva at their separate retirement residences. Or before, for that matter, when she was on call for Flora's moods. A book assigned for review by a literary quarterly lay at her bedside in the alien bedroom next to a pad attached to a clipboard, with a starting sentence on its yellow lined page. That was as much as she had managed. One sentence. Why was she sacrificing the little time left her to work? She was eighty years old, for God's sake. Was she doing it for love? Sisterhood? Was she doing it for Naomi's measly amount of money, which she was spending like water, like it grew on trees, for Naomi's good, not her own? Her own good lay north, in her house in Maine, in her life in New York with her children and grandchildren, with her friends, with her work. Would she never, ever be free of her family?

Instead of working, she swam. Miami was for swimming.

In the greeny blue of the pool on the broad terrace, out under the sky and the sun, the water heavy with chlorine, the breeze larded with the smell of fried seafood, she swam. Her body entered the water and she was sane again, agile, calmed, cured, her head clear of everything but the pleasure of free movement. She swam twice a day, avoiding the times when the pool was crowded with old Jewish men and women standing waist-high in the water chatting, or with Latino kids splashing and screaming. She swam at odd hours, alone, herself and the healing waters, one on one. In the pool she thought of a second sentence to write on the yellow lined paper, and a third, a whole paragraph. In the water's perfect embrace she was able to think.

Flora thought her mad for swimming in the pool—"That chlorine will kill you, why don't you swim in the ocean, the ocean's pure!"—when she wasn't accusing Jenny of showing off by swimming at all: "You're too old to be swimming by yourself in a pool full of chlorine. I stopped when I was eighty." It became one of their recurring struggles. She explained to Flora that she too preferred the ocean. But. There was the matter of the ridge—a couple of feet of trench filled with sharp rocks and smashed shells in a swirling undertow that unbalanced her. She would have to pass through that danger to reach swimmable waters. Couldn't Flora understand that it would be a disaster if she fell and broke a hip? She was in Miami to help, not to compound the problems. She would love to be led in and out of the dangerous trench if she could find the angel who would do that and leave her alone in between, herself and the ocean, one on one, receiving the miracle cure of the healing waters, but failing that, she would swim in the pool, reveling in the illusion of perfect mobility by way of the imperfect crawl she had been taught in high school. It was good enough. It was great. It wiped out age. For an hour or so.

The week of the scheduled move to the nursing home, Miami Beach was revving itself up for the promise of a first-class storm. The weathermen were in heaven. Their moment of glory. The word "awesome" had taken over the airwaves. Before the expected full impact, there was the menace of the blackened roiling sea beyond the condo windows, the power and the incessant noise of the astonishing wind, the sand between the teeth with every breath, on the lids and in the eyes with every blink.

Jenny had begun by pooh-poohing it all. "If you've been through a nor'easter, you've been through the worst," she said, and actually left the building, through the garage door on the side street, to buy a newspaper and prove the storm inferior.

She had exited at a moment of comparative quiet, but after a few steps, at the corner, it was impossible to stand. She sat right down on the brick path and waited for a lull, scared out of her mind, desperately clinging to the wrought-iron fence surrounding a flower bed. She watched as the entrance canopy of a seedy hotel across the street was ripped from its moorings and sent flying, a mad object of canvas and metal supports banging away at windows and the sides of buildings in a terrifying display until it touched down in front of the three-for-ten-dollars T-shirt store, knocking over the racks of sale garments perennially on sidewalk display and coming to rest wedged under a *Miami Herald* vending machine chained to a lamppost.

She crawled back into the building during the next lull and took Flora's barrage without a word of reply.

"Are you crazy? Are you crazy? What are you— *crazy?* This is a Miami Beach storm. You have no idea what we're in for. You don't tangle with a Miami Beach storm, *schvester,* not if you're in your right mind."

The danger had revived Flora. Bed no longer claimed her. She was fully dressed first thing in the morning in a bright blue Dutch boy outfit, with a middy top and pants bulging at the hips, narrowing to the ankles. She had wound around her head and throat a gossamer blue scarf, which from time to time she pulled entirely over her face, to keep the sand out, she said.

Sand was blowing into the apartment, blowing in through the tiniest exposed cracks of seams around the sills and decorative bricks, propelled by the wildly whistling wind roaring and screaming without stop. Flora was busy securing the premises, stuffing windows with cloths, piling towels on sills and on the floor along the walls facing the sea, filling pots with water, filling kettles, pitchers, jars with water, filling the refrigerator with bottles of water, filling the bathtub with water, the sinks, filling pails to place in the bathrooms in case all the other water got used up.

Though it was not yet the season, the weathermen were talking hurricane, talking hurricane-strength winds, potentially a hundred miles per hour, talking high pressure, low pressure, talking weather patterns, talking *niño*, talking direction in which the storm was moving, talking evacuation, talking eye of the storm while pointing to swirling graphics of a terrorizing nature, talking talking talking.

Flora turned on both TVs and every radio in the apartment, in case one or the other gave out. She darted around checking the refrigerator, the freezer, the cupboards. She mourned that it was too late to go to the supermarket and stock up further. She called stores that might deliver come hell or high water, found a couple, ordered two Cuban meals from one because they delivered though she didn't like Cuban food, ordered two kosher meals, chicken soup with matzo balls and noodles, roast chicken, potato kugel, kasha varnishkes, half a challa and half a rye bread, coleslaw and a couple of dill pickles, even a small sponge cake, because they delivered.

"We'll be okay," Flora said. "I stock all that canned soup and baked beans and tuna fish and gefilte fish, and there's plenty of vegetables in the crisper and frozen juice and frozen fruit in the freezer, and all that Italian stuff, pizzas and lasagna and linguine alfredo, I really love linguine alfredo, and I've got powdered milk and evaporated and even condensed because you never know, that's why I'm always stocking up, because you never know when God will decide to hit Miami Beach with everything he's got. Hey!" She was triumphant. "I just found a whole package of Hebrew National hotdogs at the back of the freezer."

Then, collapsing into laughter, "Do you remember," she said, "during the war with all the shortages, when Lionel's wife Lillian was living with us and

Lionel was in the service and Jonah was a little boy, she stuffed the closet in her bedroom with bananas because she was afraid they'd get scarce like sugar and coffee and be put on the ration books? Do you remember the stink, the awful stink of the rotting bananas and how embarrassed she was? She thought something terrible would happen to Jonah if he didn't have his mashed banana a day. She was such an idiot, God rest her soul. How in the world our brothers managed to all marry idiots is beyond me."

"What's beyond me," Jenny said, "is how that unattractive, retarded-looking, drooling baby turned into the man who's the dean of faculty at the University of Illinois, or wherever he is, and the distinguished author of half a dozen books on Freud, Jung, and Rank."

"I think it's Indiana, University of Indiana—or is that Eva's son? Who's Rank anyway? You're always coming up with these names—and the way you pronounce them. Rahnk, Rahnk," she said, mimicking the open vowel. "I'm exhausted. I have to lie down now. Could we have no more conversation for a while? Please?"

That left Jenny free to call Eva, who was napping right through the storm, according to a friend who was sitting with her in case she was scared. "And she had a real good bowel movement before she fell asleep," the friend reported.

So Eva was okay.

It was Naomi who was petrified. Naomi hadn't slept, she was in pain from the latest surgery, she couldn't find her pain pills, she hadn't been able to move her bowels, she couldn't understand why God would choose to wipe them all out here in Miami Beach on a morning when she was having trouble with her bowels.

"There's nothing, nothing but a little sand between us and the ocean. It's going to rise up in its wrath and overwhelm us. What does God think he's doing? And there's nothing we can do. Can you come here and stay with me, Jenny? Please, I'm so frightened."

Jenny, trying to remember if it was Chateaubriand who had recorded his daily bowel movements in his journals in his old age, and wondering if perhaps it was an obsession of the old generally that would overtake her any day now, heard Naomi answering herself.

"No, no, of course not, darling, it's too dangerous, don't you dare go out of the building, though

God alone knows if you'll be safe in there. I can't help it. I can't help feeling that if we're all together we're safer, if only we were all together in one place. It's been so long since we were all together in one place, safe."

Something like seventy-five years since they had all been together in one place, in the sense Naomi meant. Living together. Not partying together at weddings, bar mitzvas, big birthdays, or mourning together at funerals, and even then someone always missing, dead or ill or too busy, but *living* together. Safe? When had it been safe? Never. Too many of them, too little space in those four-room apartments, not enough bedrooms, not enough beds, too little money, too many clashing hopes, too much need, Mama overworked and torn to pieces between them, Papa centered on his sons, his sons, since the best his daughters might do was marry into prosperity, while his sons would make something of themselves, give his wasted life meaning, take care of his old age, say *Kaddish* when he died.

Daughters weren't supposed to make something of themselves, just as Mama had never made anything of herself. But what did that mean? Mama's life amounted to nothing? Of course she had made something of herself, she had made *them*, out of the calcium of her brittle bones. She had borne and raised that family whose sons Papa claimed as assets and the daughters as liabilities until they married into prosperity. Mama had worked, worked, worked. She was one of the world's great producers. She had made an extraordinary product, a human being, seven times. George Bernard Shaw believed a woman should be paid twenty thousand pounds for each child she bore, or some such sum. That would have supplied Mama with a nice little nest egg for her old age, the pension society had never granted her.

Reassuring Naomi, promising to get to Naomi just as soon as she could, she felt herself the child she had been in the midst of her family—little girl Jenny in a dream of dissimulation, doing the right thing, being good, skipping along the sidewalk on her skinny legs, skipping along in school from grade to grade without effort, caught in a monstrous enchantment of being the good little helpful unobtrusive girl to whom everything happened if not against her will then certainly without it.

My life in my family is a nightmare from which I'm

trying to awake, she paraphrased. And warned herself to stop dramatizing.

The storm veered north, offshore, lessening in power, landing without much damage on the tip of the Carolinas, dropping heavy rains along the way and leaving Miami Beach washed brilliantly clean and user-friendly, so that it became possible once again to plan Eva and Naomi's move to the nursing home.

First, manicures and pedicures had to be arranged. It started with Flora, still invigorated by the storm. She wanted to play a full part in the coming move, but first she must have a pedicure.

"And while I'm at it, I may as well have a manicure," she said.

Naomi, quite independently, said she must have a manicure and a pedicure before she went into *that place*.

And Eva, of course, had to have a pedicure and manicure too.

And while they were at it, Eva and Naomi might as well have their hair done.

For Jenny, who had never had a pedicure, and a manicure only once, when she was seventeen, for brother Max's formal wedding at Essex House on Central Park South because his wife-to-be was rich and her folks were paying and Naomi insisted that her little sister wasn't going to shame the family by attending a fancy wedding without a hair set and manicure, the whole gestalt of *manicure, pedicure* was part of the mystery of childhood, right up there with underwear and sex. Romantic sex. A permanent picture existed in her consciousness of herself as a baby, entranced by the sight and sweet smell of grown-up glamorous Eva dressed in a pink brocade gown, sitting at the window of the family's crowded Brooklyn flat, polishing her nails with a long silver-handled shammy buffer. Eva was waiting for the arrival of the man she was to become engaged to that night. He would take her out to dinner in a swanky restaurant (Italian), where he would formally propose and present her with a diamond engagement ring (small). Jenny learned all this later from Flora, who was talented at ferreting out family secrets. But hidden in the romance of the pink brocade and the shining nails was something else, something dark to do with expensive silken underwear and partial violent nakedness, something shuddery to do with the tall, handsome, forbidding man in a tuxedo who was the manager of the office where soft-skinned, soft-eyed big sister Eva worked as a bookkeeper and had nabbed this good catch that Papa was so pleased with. And hidden in her older sister's hope was thick, dispiriting dread, so pervasive that Jenny smelled it on Eva's skin. Eva was not quite eighteen years old.

Eventually the diamond ring would be pawned and lost in one of Eva's husband's recurring disastrous slides into financial failure during their long marriage. The silver-handled buffer survived the ring, tarnishing a bit along with its matching hand mirror and comb and brush that sat on a silver tray on Eva's dresser wherever Eva's dresser turned up throughout the economic vagaries of her marriage, until the old-fashioned set finally disappeared out of Eva's life.

And the painted nails survived, the shining painted fingernails of her sisters as they grew up ahead of her. The smell of the nail polish and the remover over the smell of their perfume was embedded in Jenny's memories like the smell of dill in Mama's Friday night chicken soup, but while Mama's dill insured love and safety, nail polish sent a different message, of soft hidden flesh in the silky underwear they bought even when they couldn't afford it, for the naked struggles with the men they did or didn't catch, to equal disaster. Eva caught her office manager and stayed married all her life. Naomi lost out on her first love—gave herself to him like a fool, as she always put it, and then lost him—finally caught a husband, found him tasteless, let the marriage be annulled, went on to other lovers, found a final husband who had the good grace to die soon, went on with her varied secret love life. And then there was Flora.

There wasn't enough distance between herself and Flora for glamour to enter. Flora was only five years older, and even when she started to paint her nails, there was no mystery about underwear. She wore the same kind of cotton bloomers Jenny did—a little larger—and it never occurred to Jenny that Flora might wear her bloomers with a difference until she was enlightened by a mutual friend up the block in the Bronx. The friend was older than Jenny, a little younger than twelve-year-old Flora. The friend's name was Friend, Dorothy Friend, and she shared a room with her only brother, Bernie Friend, who was six years older.

"I do it with my brother. Bernie does it to me all

the time," Dorothy Friend said, and watched Jenny closely to observe the effect. Disappointed at seeing none she could decipher on the carefully blank face, she tried again. "And Flora and your brother do it all the time too."

Jenny was standing next to Dorothy in the bedroom Dorothy and Bernie Friend had shared all their lives. To Jenny, used to the makeshift sleeping arrangements of not enough rooms and too many brothers and sisters, its furnishings were impressive: a regular bedroom set—twin beds, double dresser, night tables, matching spreads—school diplomas on the wall, family photographs, a framed embroidered square announcing "God Lives in Our Hearts." Not even Mama and Papa had a real bedroom like this one.

Jenny thought, *Which bed do they do it in? What is "it," anyway, and where in our hopelessly crowded apartment are Flora and Max doing "it"?* She desperately needed to flee that bedroom and Dorothy Friend's greedy eyes, waiting to lap up her shock. She wasn't going to grant Dorothy that victory.

"I know all about it," she said airily. "I have to go home now." And ran.

Did she believe Dorothy Friend? Yes. Back at

her own tenement stoop, her heart beating painfully, she admitted that she knew it was true. She had blocked all Flora's hints, pretended that she had dreamed her favorite brother's night roamings naked under a draped sheet, pretended that she didn't know what Flora and Max were doing in Mama and Papa's tiny back bedroom with the door closed when only the three of them were in the apartment on those nights when Mama and Papa worked late at the store and nobody else was home. Was she horrified? No, she was jealous. Not that she really wanted to be in the room with Flora and Max, but she didn't want to be shut out either. She didn't know what she wanted. She hated Flora's special position, she hated Flora washing her bloomers in the bathroom basin, gasping, scrubbing, yelling at Jenny as tears fell into the soapy water. "Get out of here. You're just a baby. You don't know anything. Stop watching me. Babies can't watch."

What Jenny remembers, shuddering at herself, is that she blamed Flora, not brother Max. It was all Flora's fault—she shouldn't have let Max into her bloomers, and she shouldn't have called Jenny a baby. If she had been a loyal sister she would have insisted on including Jenny in whatever went on in the back bedroom. Then none of "it" would have happened.

And now? Now she wants to beg Flora's forgiveness for not being on Flora's side all the way. "I *was* a baby," she wants to say to Flora, "what could I have done?"

What she did was to follow her sisters' leads more or less blindly, though without the nail polish. She constructed her own version of manicures and pedicures, her own rules of bloomers, panties, silk underwear and nakedness and the twining of arms and legs culminating in the glorious spasms of transcendent warmth right down to her unpainted toes. But she owed her sisters. They had given her a lot. She owed her sisters' lives, her mother's life, for preparing her, badly, for the field of battle she would enter behind them. Remember, remember, she had told herself over and over again, don't make their mistakes, make your own, create a different battlefield, and if you fail you'll have fallen in a war where others may succeed, daughters and granddaughters, nieces and great-nieces, the women who come after.

And of course she had failed, failed to put together love heart soul mind sex friendship equality family community—arid, stupid words for the search that had governed her life. A good search, take it all in all, failure or not. Did the search itself add up to a good life? She had done her best, had flexed her tiny muscle and fought the good fight. Had she won anything? It felt as if she had. Was this the way everyone felt at the end, that they had won something valuable and enduring, in spite, in spite of the defeats?

She made the arrangements for the manicures and pedicures, Flora's at the corner beauty parlor run by Russian Jews newly arrived from Moscow and Leningrad, known once again as St. Petersburg; Eva's at her residence, where a manicurist/pedicurist regularly took care of the women; and Naomi's by arrangement with the Russian émigré from Flora's beauty parlor, who was willing to make the trip for forty-five dollars plus cab fare.

Flora argued that it was ridiculous to pay all that money. "Naomi can make it to the beauty parlor if she tries," she said. "You'll save at least fifteen dollars if she gets to the beauty parlor, and she can do it if she really tries. Look at me, I'm still in there fighting, and I can't tell you how weak I feel, horribly horribly weak. I don't know how I manage to keep moving, I don't know how

I keep going, but I do, and so could Naomi if only she wouldn't give up."

"Yes, but with the wheelchair and taxis I'll spend fifteen dollars getting her to the salon, so it's six of one and half a dozen of the other," Jenny said.

"Where'd you pick that up, 'six of one and half a dozen of the other'?"

"It's a common expression. Everybody uses it, or they used to."

But Flora continued to gaze at Jenny angrily. Once again she had infuriated Flora without knowing why.

In the end, strapped into their wheelchairs in the medical van, Eva and Naomi looked fine, their pretty hair nicely done, Eva's short and slightly mannish, Naomi's with its sweet part and simple arrangement, Naomi charming in a printed flowing skirt and matching top, a dark wool throw over her shoulders because she was always cold, and a straw topper in her hand if needed against the glare of the sun, Eva elegant in an all-black pantsuit with a beautifully pleated white silk blouse, black patent sandals, and a matching purse, their fingernails gleaming red on the pocketbooks clutched in their laps, their painted toenails shining red through their open-toed sandals.

Jenny had arranged for the van to arrive first at Naomi's residence and then travel north along the beach to Eva's residence, and from there south again over causeways toward the city of Miami and to the nursing home. Jenny and Flora were to get to Naomi's on their own, Jenny naturally thinking of a cab but Flora insisting on a bus ride. Jenny was too worn out and preoccupied to argue.

Flora had outfitted herself in a casual purple linen pantsuit, her hair curling out of a little purple cap worn far back on her head, a purple scarf at her throat, an oversized purple bag slung on her shoulder. She listed sideways with its weight, leaning heavily on Jenny for support, shuffling along in her purple sandals, the bright red toenails shining.

"Too much, too much." Once seated in the bus Flora heaved great deep sighs, intoning, "Too much, too much, too much to bear." She threw back her head and gasped for air, stretching her remarkably shapely limbs ending in the purple sandals into the aisle of the bus. Other passengers looked at her with pitying sympathy and eyed Jenny coldly for just sitting there, not paying sufficient attention to her ailing sister.

The bus left them close to Naomi's residence. They could see the medical van already parked in the circular driveway, and Naomi in her wheelchair at the door with a group of fellow residents gathered around her.

"Don't tell them anything," Naomi whispered desperately. "They think I'm going to the hospital for some tests. Don't tell them, don't tell them anything."

Everybody knew the truth, of course, down to the tiniest detail. They had seen Naomi's packed suitcases leaving the residence in the beat-up station wagon that Luis the Cuban night clerk used for odd jobs he picked up now and then, and of course Luis told everybody everything he knew. And the residents gossiped among themselves: they knew where Naomi was going, everybody knew that her dying sister Eva was going into the home too, everybody knew that it was the last place for both, everybody knew it was the end of the line for Naomi. They kissed and hugged her, murmuring vague loving wishes. "I hope everything goes well for you, I'll never forget you, it's been wonderful knowing you,

God be with you, God bless, God bless." They turned away with tears in their eyes, for Naomi and for themselves, for their own last journey.

Shimon, the retired professor, kissed Naomi's hand over and over again, holding out a small orchid corsage "just for nothing, just for your loveliness, just for the great pleasure of knowing you." Jenny pinned it to the shoulder of Naomi's dark wool throw because Shimon was too deaf to hear Naomi suggesting that he do so. Naomi held her head up, her humped back as straight as she could make it, her eyes smiling, her manner gracious, pretending that the true event that was happening wasn't happening at all.

Flora stayed inside, chatting with the residents, filling them in on further details about the home, keeping them out of the way while the complicated drama of moving Naomi into the vehicle staged itself. Outside in the sun, the heat struck with violence. As if handling an unwieldy package, two very large glum white men carried Naomi and the wheelchair down the short flight of stairs at the entrance. Naomi had put on the little straw topper, its gay tilt incongruous in the circumstances.

The men parked Naomi in the driveway while

they lowered a platform on the vehicle, a maneuver accompanied by an alarming muttering grinding noise. When they placed Naomi on the platform in her wheelchair, she reached out in terror for Jenny's hand. Shaking, Jenny scrambled up beside Naomi, stroking her, making stupid jokes. The platform rose, muttering and grinding, to the level of the vehicle's floor. Naomi closed her eyes, dark and clouded now in the yellowish white of her skin. The men wrestled the chair to the far end of the large, gloomy van, where to Jenny's horror she saw that Eva had already been locked in.

"Jenny," Eva said, and burst into uncontrollable weeping. "Damn it, where have you been? Why did my kids leave this all to you? I told them, I told them I can't depend on my sisters."

"You were supposed to pick her up last, after this pickup. After. After!" Jenny was yelling, almost crying herself, furious that her carefully plotted scenario had been ruined.

The men paid no attention, busy with leather straps and chains to immobilize the wheelchair safely. They slammed doors, shot bolts, a sound of prison clatter. Eva cried. Naomi moaned and covered her eyes with a trembling long-fingered manicured hand.

"Oh please, no fights, let's not fight, please," she whispered.

"There you are, all set," the bigger man said. And to outraged Jenny, "Sorry, didn't make sense to go north, then south, then north again. They changed the route, it made more sense." He left to secure the back doors from the outside.

Jenny knelt between her sisters, murmuring, kissing, making more stupid jokes, begging Eva's forgiveness, explaining how it was not supposed to have gone as it did. This damned mix-up had turned her into a child again.

"It's like going to the guillotine or the electric chair, for God's sake," Naomi said. "You have to stay with us in this ambulance, Jenny, or whatever it is, this tumbrel. Don't let them make you leave us." Characteristically, she made this plea with her head down and to the side, as if she herself had nothing to do with this other gibbering being.

Eva brought her tears to a gargling stop. "Forgive me," she said. "I don't want to act like a baby, but when they treat you like a goddamn baby . . . Let's just get this over with as quickly as possible." Suddenly she was oldest sister Eva dispensing marks for good conduct. "Jenny, you look lovely, dear, that cream-colored silk is beautiful." And then, again in a horrified child's panic, "Are you leaving us?"

"Just for a minute, I'm just going out for a minute to get Flora," Jenny said. "I'll be right back, Eva, Naomi, right right back."

She charged up to the drivers, who were standing on the steps of the residence filling in papers on a clipboard. She could see Flora sitting inside, gesticulating broadly, talking, talking.

"Excuse me, but on the phone with your dispatcher I told him quite clearly that we would be staying with our sisters throughout." Jenny made her demand sound briskly inevitable. "It's bad enough that you picked up my older sister first. That wasn't the plan."

"No problem," the balder of the two men answered. "You can ride up front near us."

The bigger man added, "Just make it quick, okay? We don't want to spend all day on one pickup."

They were both dressed in dark blue guards' uniforms complete with medical insignia, but Jenny recognized regular truckers underneath.

Then the big one spoke again. "They're okay, your sisters are okay, they all get a little scared 'cause of the safety lockup, but they get used to it. Could you hurry it up, lady, we've got another call on our books."

Jenny waved frantically to Flora. "Come on, we have to go!"

It was the more kindly driver who strapped Jenny and Flora into the passenger seat, a narrow wooden bench under a small window behind the front seat, but the restraints were merely elaborate safety belts—no rattling chains, no bolts, no metal tracks.

"Y'know, we're liable if anybody gets hurt in our vehicle, so we have to be careful," he said, and pulled the heavy side door shut.

In the dark cool of the air conditioning, with eerie streaks of light arching from the little window separating them from the drivers, Jenny heard more prison clatter of bolts fastened, a door being opened and slammed shut, garbled conversation between the two men, the motor starting up. They were in motion, on their way to the last destination for Eva and Naomi, proceeding slowly in the heavy traffic on Collins. They were all silent. Flora seemed to be praying, her head lolling on her chest, her legs outstretched. Eva sat rigidly, her eyes fixed on nothing. Naomi covered her face with her hands, her painted nails shining in the half darkness.

My sisters, my self, Jenny thought. *I love you as myself*. What could she do to protect them from this unspeakable reality? And herself?

Flora began a chanting poem. "'My love came up from Barnegat with thunder in his eyes, my love came up from Barnegat telling terrible lies . . .'"

"No, no," Eva objected. "No poetry, please."

"Let's sing," Jenny said, "let's sing," and in a quavering whisper began, "'Good night, Irene, good night, Irene, I'll see you in my dreams . . .'"

"Too tame," Flora said, interrupting in her strong, true voice. "'And when the saints go marching in, and when the saints go marching in . . .'"

"Isn't it 'come marching in'?" Naomi corrected, and joined Flora, her voice strengthening with each note.

Eva's addition was more of a croak, but she clapped her hands and swung her feet as if she were marching. And when Jenny threw her voice into the mix, Flora took off on a harmonizing riff, banging the flat of her hand against the wooden bench, keeping the beat strong for the others.

Still singing, Jenny turned to peer out the front window through a little aperture in the partition. They were approaching the Fontainebleau. Above them the huge *trompe l'oeil* loomed and beckoned, a Fontainebleau where nothing ever changed, where they would live forever in splendid rooms, elegantly dressed, hair done, nails polished on hands and feet, wrapped in music, surrounded by boutiques, coffee shops, restaurants, bars, in an Eden of benign ocean and wide beach, outdoor pool and indoor gym, of gardens in lush bloom, and overarching all, the unchanging brilliant blue sky. If only the awful vehicle could rise, effortlessly sail upward and deposit them all in the perfection of the painted Fontainebleau: a trick of the eye magically transforming the sisters' shared, searching, stumbling steps into a triumphant escape from the real horrors to come. But the van, grounded to the pavement, steadily took the curve that would carry them to Eva and Naomi's final home, and in time, Flora's, and in one way or another, Jenny's too.

Acknowledgments

For their help, I want to thank my friends Doris Grumbach and Vivian Gornick; my agents, Frances Goldin and Sydelle Kramer; my publishers, Cecile Engel and Lori Milken; and my editor, Joy Johannessen, for her meticulous care of the text.